Music in American Life

A list of books in the series appears at the end of this book.

HEARTLAND
EXCURSIONS

HEARTLAND EXCURSIONS

*Ethnomusicological Reflections
on Schools of Music*

∾   BRUNO NETTL   ∾

UNIVERSITY OF ILLINOIS PRESS / URBANA AND CHICAGO

© 1995 by the Board of Trustees of the University of Illinois
Manufactured in the United States of America
P   6   5   4   3   2

This book is printed on acid-free paper.

Library of Congress Cataloging-in-Publication Data
Nettl, Bruno, 1930–
    Heartland excursions : ethnomusicological reflections on schools
of music / Bruno Nettl.
        p.   cm. — (Music in American life)
    Includes index.
        ISBN 0-252-06468-2 (pbk.) / ISBN 978-0-252-06468-5 (pbk.)
    1. Music in universities and colleges—United States. 2. Musical
canon. 3. Ethnomusicology. I. Series.
MT18.N48   1995
780'.89—dc20   94-18625
                                                              CIP
                                                              MN

For Wanda,
the lady of my life,
and
for my granddaughter,
Natalie

Contents

Preface

In classes about the musical cultures of Iran, of the Blackfoot people, and of Madras, I have normally used comparisons with Western classical music culture as an instructional technique and point of departure, and so it may have been inevitable that I would at some point start out with perspectives of other musical cultures in trying to gain insight into the classical music culture in contemporary America. The idea for a book on this subject first came to me when Daniel Neuman, in 1984, suggested that we read, Huntley-Brinkley style, a joint paper titled "The Ethnomusicological Study of Western Culture," and so I wish to express special thanks to Dan for having once almost come to the point of participating in the writing of these chapters, and then encouraging me to go it alone, on a subject that many of my colleagues considered outré, to say the least. I have had occasion to try out parts of the chapters as lectures on various audiences and received many helpful and critical responses. Some thought I wasn't serious, remembering best my throwing a few pieces of the delicious candy known as *Mozartkugeln,* or Mozart balls, into the audience at a strategic point, while elsewhere it was assumed (with some delight) that my political agenda was requiring me to stick it to traditionalist music professors. At one university a colleague praised, but with a bit of disbelief, "It's, oh, so *radical,*" and at another my host, warned that I might be controversial or even hard to take, exclaimed, "Oh, if only we could occasionally have a musicology lecture which *someone* would find offensive!"

Now, almost ten years after I began this project (which first grew and then shrank in scope and ambition), the ethnomusicological study of Western culture is taken for granted by most ethnomusicologists and is even no longer outré to other music scholars. My purpose is certainly not to be radical or outrageous. Rather, I wish to pay homage to what I consider to be my own musical culture, and to the kind of institution in which I have spent most of my life, by studying it as I have tried to study other musical systems that I also admire and to see whether what I have learned in other cultures may be helpful in understanding my own.

For help received in the course of working on this manuscript I am grateful to many—more, alas, than I can list. But let me mention at least a few: Eugene Giles, Daniel M. Neuman, Ellen Koskoff, and Helen Myers read the entire manuscript at various stages of completion. Many others have read portions, or discussed the problems with me, or responded to lectures on the subjects of the book and made helpful suggestions; among them, I want to thank Carol Babiracki, Paul Berliner, Steve Blum, Phil Bohlman, Charlie Capwell, Austin Clarkson, Rich Crawford, Steve Fiol, Janet Keller, Tammy Livingston, Vicki Levine, James Porter, Melinda Russell, Zohreh Sullivan, Anne Swartz, Tom Turino, Larry Ward, Isabel Wong, and Chris Waterman. I appreciate the advice and support of all these colleagues more than I can say.

Included at various points in this volume are revised and expanded versions of ideas and interpretations published elsewhere in article form. Earlier versions of some sections of chapters 1, 3, and 4 were published in "Heartland Excursions: Exercises in Musical Ethnography" in *The World of Music: Journal of the Institute for Traditional Music,* volume 34, number 1 (Wilhelmshaven: Florian Noetzel Verlag, 1992). Some sections of chapters 1, 2, and 3 are revised versions of parts of my article "Mozart and the Ethnomusicological Study of Western Culture," which appeared in *Yearbook for Traditional Music,* volume 21, edited by Dieter Christensen in 1989. In chapters 1 and 3, I also present revisions of several paragraphs published in my essay "A Place for All Music? The Concentric Circles of the Music Building," which appeared in *Community of Music: An Ethnographic Seminar in Champaign-Urbana,* edited by Tamara E. Livingston, Melinda Russell, Larry F. Ward, and I (Champaign: Elephant and Cat, 1993). A still earlier version of that essay appears in *Music-Cultures in Contact: Convergences and Collisions,* edited by Margaret Kartomi and Stephen Blum (Melbourne: Currency Press, 1994). I am grateful to the editors and publishers of these earlier versions for permission to include the revised sections here.

Finally, thanks to my long-time friend and editor Judy McCulloh; to Tony Seeger, who read the manuscript for the University of Illinois Press; and to my wife Wanda for seeing me through yet another project.

HEARTLAND
EXCURSIONS

Introduction

Ethnomusicology at Home

Let me be quite personal. What is it about ethnomusicology that has fascinated me over some four decades? At first, it was the opportunity of looking at something quite strange, of hearing totally unexpected musical sounds and experiencing thoroughly unfamiliar ideas about music. Later, to learn to look at any of the world's cultures, and listen to any of the musics, without being judgmental. And further on, the notion that one should find ways of comprehending an entire musical culture, identifying its central paradigms, and finding points of entry, or perhaps handles, for grasping a culture or capturing a music. And eventually, also having practiced the outsider's view, to look also at the familiar as if it were not, at one's own culture as if one were a foreigner to it. Evidently these are points that have also fascinated some of my colleagues; in their order they seem to me to reflect something of the history of ethnomusicology since 1950. This volume belongs to the latest of these stages.

One of the principal topics at a major international conference of ethnomusicologists in 1993 was "ethnomusicology at home," an indication that ethnomusicologists are officially ready to turn to the contemplation of their own societies. But that topic is not so new. After all, scholars who identified themselves as ethnomusicologists and who were Africans, Indians, Native Americans, and Indonesians have all along been studying the music of their own cultural backyards. And for some time, the study of urban minorities in the cities of North America and

Europe, typical dwelling places of ethnomusicologists, has been a major activity. Some ethnomusicologists have also (after decades of resistance, to be sure) come to accept the study of popular music and the vernacular repertories of their own communities.

Ethnomusicology is variously defined. But most ethnomusicologists regard their field as capable of casting light on all sorts and types of music, and they have gradually widened their scope to include, in practice as well as theory, a world of repertories and cultures and subcultures, including the ethnomusicology of "home." Just what "home" may be, in a complex society, and to what extent the consideration of one individual's musical culture is more than idiosyncrasy are issues for debate. But in the last two decades, ethnomusicologists have finally expanded their net to capture (with mixed metaphors) the last bastion of unstudied musical culture, Western classical music, especially as it exists in the contemporary world

Unstudied? This musical culture that has been worked over by thousands of music historians, critics, sociologists, and music theorists? Is it possible that the vantage point of ethnomusicology could add anything of interest? A small number of my colleagues (some of whom might actually not wish to be called ethnomusicologists) have indeed made such contributions. My purpose is not to provide a bibliographical survey, but among those whose recent works come to mind are Christopher Small, Judith Becker, Catherine Cameron, Ruth Finnegan, Pierre Bourdieu, and most important for this study, Henry Kingsbury, whose dissertation was based mainly on detailed observations of a major East Coast conservatory.[1]

One asks in what way the research of these authors fits into the specific framework of ethnomusicology, what they have done that might not be done by members of other disciplines or subdisciplines. Ethnomusicologists have contributed to the understanding of the classical music culture of our century in several ways: They try to comprehend the musical culture through a microcosm, to provide an even-handed appraisal without judgment, to look was well as possible at the familiar as if one were an outsider, to see the world of music as a component of culture in the anthropological sense of that word, and to view their own music from a world perspective.[2]

Here I hope to participate in this branch of ethnomusicological endeavor by analyzing and commenting upon some important aspects of Western art music culture from these various perspectives. I have been trying to do "ethnomusicology at home."

Heartland Music Schools

"Home" for me is schools of music in universities in the Midwest, particularly the southern Midwest, the heartland of America, as some residents would have it. These are constituent units in their institutions, usually called "schools of music" but sometimes "departments of music" as well; they are frequently headed by administrators who are directly under general university officers such as chancellors or provosts. They have this in common: In contrast with typical music departments in liberal arts colleges, which usually teach only music history, theory, and composition along with the maintenance of orchestra, band, and chorus, they emphasize the teaching of performance—instruments and voice—as well as composition and the pedagogical and scholarly aspects of music. They concentrate not only on the education of music specialists but also provide instruction for students in other fields and concerts and ceremonial music at everything from football games and commencements to formal concerts. But the "music" in schools of music always means, exclusively or overwhelmingly, Western classical music (also called "art music," "canonic music," "cultivated music," "serious music," and even—wryly—"real music" and "normal music"). Schools of music are ordinarily divided into homogeneous units. Sometimes there are only two—the departments of performance study and of academic studies and composition. More commonly there are several: strings, winds, piano, voice, musicology, composition, and music education, for example. The ways in which the school's teachers and students are subdivided is one of the abiding issues in many schools. Major components of any school of music are ensembles that give periodic public performances—the university orchestra, one or several bands, choruses, and more.

It seems appropriate to provide a brief characterization of the kind of institution with which I deal, and much more will be observed about its structure, the relationships of its components, and the rules and customs under which it lives. I am, however, not describing particular individual schools or a specific group of schools. I attempt, rather, to identify, discuss, and interpret some important values and guiding principles in the world of Western art music in the United States and in the way it is taught and transmitted, using a type of institution as a point of entry to the culture. I draw on information from many sources and from experience at many institutions in a period of fifty years of mu-

sic study and teaching, a half-century spent almost entirely at midwestern schools of music. Most of my experience and observations have
come since the seventies—although I sometimes reach back to my early
observations in the late 1940s—and the principal venues are the University of Illinois and Indiana University. To a much smaller extent, I
learned things at the University of Louisville, somewhat less at the
University of Michigan and Wayne State University, and a bit from
Millikin University. And a good deal of what I have learned comes, as
well, from a large number of other major institutions throughout the
nation, most of them schools of music at major state universities. Writ-
ings about the field of music in higher education and special studies of
individual schools such as Kingsbury's provide more information and
some corroboration.

Some of my reflections result from many years of observing concerts, rehearsals, and lessons; counting people in audiences, types of
pieces on programs, and various kinds of faculty in departments and
institutions; and having literally thousands of conversations about the
issues presented here with hundreds of musicians, teachers, and students. I have also supervised the gathering of systematic data by students in seminars.[3] But ethnomusicologists in the field, in addition
to systematic data gathering, recording, conducting interviews, and
counting, make many observations through informal and random
contact, conversation, noticing, and making connections in their
minds, and they gain from this perhaps intuitive technique some of
the most significant aspects of their perception and presentation. Thus,
more important, I believe, is my involvement over five decades with
music schools, an involvement also informed by my experience in
other cultures.

My purpose is not to provide hard data about curricula, performances, or personnel. Rather, I would like to impart my personal
understanding and reflections on the flavor of the internal interrelationships of the groups of people—and perhaps the groups of musics—that constitute and populate music schools. Throughout, I refer to a fictitious "Heartland U.," an abstracted combination of the
institutions mentioned earlier. In order to avoid offending the many
colleagues, students, and friends from whom I have learned and
whom I have observed, I have consciously avoided, most of the time,
discussing and naming specific universities, departments, or individuals and have tried to generalize my illustrations. This is not an "eth-

nographie à clef." Nor does it provide the comprehensive coverage of a traditional ethnography, supported by data gathered as specific times and places and documented for replication and verification. But I do hope to contribute to ethnographic literature by attempting to relate schools of music and the complex of structures and ideas that govern them to the modern Western culture of which they are a part.

Four Perspectives

I have tried to look through the Heartland U. music school (or schools) from four perspectives. The first, "In the Service of the Masters" (chapter 1), views it as something like a religious system or a social system in which both living and deceased participate. In my observation, the average member of music school society, asked to describe the Western art music, is likely to say that it is the music of the great composers—Beethoven, Bach, Mozart, Schubert—and that it is most essentially great works for large performing forces—operas, concertos, and symphonies. It makes sense to think of the music school, therefore, as a society ruled by deities with sacred texts, rituals, ceremonial numbers, and a priesthood.

The second perspective, "Society of Musicians" (chapter 2), examines the ways in which members of music school society group themselves into sets of opposing forces: teachers, students, and administrators; performers and academics; strings and winds; singers and players; and, most important, conductors and conducted. The tensions and alliances among these groups and the importance of hierarchies reflect analogous characteristics in American society.

The third perspective, "A Place for All Musics" (chapter 3), shows the music school as a venue for the meeting of potentially all musics, discusses the ways in which they mix, as in a melting pot, or retain their separate identities, as in a mosaic, and draws a parallel between the interrelationship of musics in the music school and the interaction of cultures in the global society of the twentieth century.

The fourth perspective, "Forays into the Repertory" (chapter 4), looks at some ways in which music school society interprets the body of Western classical music with which it works. I examine the shape of the repertory by seeking a center that may consist of ceremonial songs or of the traditional canon of masterworks; by suggesting that music school society sees its musical repertory as a kind of society of

its own, with a variety of functions and interactions; and by outlin-
ing one type of event whose purpose seems to be to use musical sound
and behavior to define concepts such as power, art, and musicianship. In all of this discussion, I have tried to retain a vestige of the
intercultural comparative perspective that I consider essential to ethnomusicology, and I have done so in part by providing comparisons
with other cultures from which I have learned, particularly those of
the Blackfoot people, the musicians of Tehran, and the Carnatic music
masters of Madras.

Inspirations

This volume does not presume to be anthropology nor is it really traditional ethnomusicology, but in the preparation of its chapters
I have been greatly influenced and inspired by some standard ethnomusicological and anthropological literature and feel that an account
of the most important works may help readers understand, in collo-
quial terms, "where I am coming from." Alas, there are too many
authors and publications to which I should pay homage, but I will
list the most essential. Inspiration they have been, but I do not wish
to suggest that I have been able to do a comprehensive job of following in their footsteps.

From the first book of anthropology I ever read, Ruth Benedict's
Patterns of Culture, I learned that one significant way to comprehend
a culture is to find dominant themes that exhibit themselves in a
variety of cultural domains and behavior patterns.[4] I have tried to find
such themes, for example, when I suggest that the opposition between
inspiration and disciplined labor is one of the driving forces of music schools. Bronislaw Malinowski's work provides one of the earliest, and also one of the clearest, outlines for ethnographic study in
its exhortation to field workers—in addition to the collecting of formal structures ("customary behavior associated with focal institutions") and texts ("corpus inscriptionum")—to make minute, detailed
observations of the ways people behave and interact, and thus to note
what he calls "the imponderabilia of everyday life."[5] These kinds of
observation were often among the most satisfying considerations for
me. I should also mention Clifford Geertz's classic description of one
event, the Balinese cockfight, as a performance indicative of many
salient features and major principles of Balinese culture.[6] Here, I

describe a couple of events that I felt had this kind of significance, such as the music school commencement, but I do so much less comprehensively than Geertz. The use of myth as a principal "handle" on culture was developed most clearly by Claude Lévi-Strauss in several works and, for musical culture, by Steven Feld's work on the Kaluli.[7] I look at music building society through the myths about great composers that permeate it. The suggestion that for the study of a complex culture with a classical music system one can perhaps gain most by examining the social relationships among musicians and the way in which they transmit the music and its values is significantly articulated in Daniel Neuman's book on musicians in Delhi.[8] I also view music school society as a group of cooperating and conflicting populations.

Ethnomusicological literature naturally has provided many models and influences. One of the most significant is Alan Merriam's classic musical ethnography of the Flathead Indians, still one of the best comprehensive treatments of the musical culture of a numerically small society, although it fails to realize one of its author's principal aims, to connect the study of musical sound and the study of music in culture.[9] Merriam's insistence, throughout his career, of studying societies small enough to make comprehensive understanding a possibility gave direction to a number of works, among them Anthony Seeger's *Why Suyá Sing,* a study of a society of some 150 people whose musical culture is so complex that one can only begin to comprehend it through analysis of a few salient aspects.[10] I perceive the society of the music building as small but complex, a bit like some tribal societies perhaps, isolated in some ways and not in others.

James Clifford happily uses a musical term *polyphonic* to suggest that the relationship of a society to its culture ought to be described in a variety of voices reflecting the differential views of observers and participants and questioning the validity of a single authority and any coherent system that anyone can impose on the innumerable things that comprise a culture.[11] Readers may be struck by the many groups, the number of organizations, and the variety of musics that comprise a Heartland music school. Although I rarely quote directly the views of the people with whom I conversed or from whom I learned, I do try to show that music building society is not monolithic and could be best understood if perceived from different vantage points. This I try to do by assuming three voices. Sometimes I am simply speaking as an ethnomusicologist teaching at Heartland U. and writing a conventional account. Frequently, I am also the principal native informant who has lived in Heartland's music school culture for many years and knows its ins and outs as well as anyone. Finally, I try to see the music school as an outsider would, remembering my experiences as an outsider in other cultures and the questions I asked to help me get insight. For this, I introduce the legendary "ethnomusicologist from Mars" who comes to the Heartlands with no knowledge and thus experiences everything from scratch. I won't label the approach taken in each paragraph or section, but I hope to combine and alternate these three author's roles beneficially.

Don't Forget: It's My Music

The central question of ethnomusicology, it seems to me, is why a particular society has its particular music and musical culture.[12] It is a question that is rarely broached in its general sense, but much ethnomusicological literature is directed to it, at least by implication. If there is any agreement in the scholarly population on this point, it must be that something about the nature, the character, of a society's culture determines what kind of music it has. It would be tempting to say that we must look to fundamental values and principles of Western culture for an explanation of the great value of large ensembles, the importance of hierarchy in many aspects of the classical music system, and the emphasis on polyphony. The situation is too complex for me to promise success, but one of my principal aims is contribute to its discussion.

Among the complications are issues that Merriam and Neuman raise. Neuman suggests that music does three things for cultures, or rather, that societies use music to do three things for them. To elaborate Neuman's statements, music is a functioning part of culture, one of the domains that contribute to the culture complex; it is also a microcosm of culture whose structures, relationships, and events it reflects.[13] But also it is a commentary on culture. Taking the third of these functions literally, we can see that musical life and musical structure may reflect, contradict, parody, exaggerate, soften, and idealize the stuff of everyday life. A wonderful musical system may not mean a wonderful cultural system, only the desire for one; a musical system with sharp social distinctions may reflect such a social system, or it may only remind us that the social system contains the seeds of inequality.

Merriam suggests that in many cultures, including that of twentieth-century America, music is (to a degree) the province of social deviants and thus often exists, as it were, to contradict what the culture is otherwise saying.[14] My own attempts to relate cultural structures to musical structures and, in turn, to structures of musical society should be viewed in the light of contradictory or multiple functions of music and with firm skepticism. "It ain't necessarily so." Thus, I repeat: This is my view, a view based on ethnomusicological experience and approaches, but my own interpretation.

Readers may find much of what I say to be explicitly or, probably more likely, implicitly critical. Criticism, however, is not my purpose. To be sure, in my experience members of many societies, confronted with an outsider's uncritical analysis of their culture, tend to read into the analysis a critical intent. If I motivate those readers who regard themselves as cultural insiders of my mythical Heartland U. music school to seek change, so be it. In my everyday life, I would be one of them. But for the purpose of this book I wish to remove myself from that role, much as I have also tried my best to remain outside the fray in my observations of other musics.

The music whose culture I am discussing is "my" music and "my" culture in the most specific sense. It is the first music I heard, the music with which I grew up, and which, in the aggregate, I have heard most often throughout my life, and so I really am doing "ethnomusicology at home" to a perhaps unprecedented degree. I believe that my musical culture can withstand, as can the society of its music schools, some analytical discussion that may have critical implications.

Although I may discuss Western classical music—and the subculture that practices and teaches it in one of its twentieth-century venues—with a raised forefinger, or with tongue in cheek, or with wrinkled nose, and maybe even with a note of cynicism or sarcasm, and although I think that it may reflect the cultural structure of a sometimes mean and unkind society, I nevertheless cannot imagine life without it.

∾ 1 ∾

In the Service of the Masters

Scholar from Mars

An extraterrestrial ethnomusicologist from Mars arrives at the midwestern school of music and begins work by listening to conversations, reading concert programs, and eavesdropping at rehearsals, lessons, and performances. The E.T. is overwhelmed by hearing a huge number of names of persons, but eventually it realizes that many of these persons are alive, but many others are no longer living and yet the rhetoric treats them similarly. "Let's go and listen to George," she overhears, and, later, "Let's go and hear Beethoven." And another time, "Nobody can handle voicing like Brahms," but also, "There's no one who has a tone like Ms. Winter." The next day: "That year is a low point in Bruckner's career, but later on he is again much more authoritative," but in the afternoon, "I heard Mr. Farina's latest work, and he sure is on a roll this year." He is tempted to mix earthly metaphors and suggest that in the Music Building you can't tell the quick from the dead without a program.

The E.T. soon finds that many kinds of figures populate the school: students, teachers, administrators, members of audiences, musicians who are not present but who are known, and a large number of musicians who are not living but are treated as friends in conversation. Among these are a few who seem to be the dominant figures in the school. They constitute pantheon, the composers about whom one rarely if ever hears a critical word. Two seem to get more (well, perhaps just a tiny bit more) attention than the rest; their names are Mozart and Beethoven, and they appear to have the roles of chief deities.

The ethnomusicologist from Mars sees that one approach to understanding the culture of the Music Building would be to find out how it is that the great composers, particularly Mozart and Beethoven, dominate the realm and what values or concepts in society this dominance suggests. As it happens, the E.T. arrived on earth in 1991, and so the figure of Mozart, on the bicentennial of his death, stands out. If one were to ask the nation's music lovers to name the most famous composer, many would give Mozart or Beethoven. If one were to ask musicians to think hard and then to name the most "normal" Western composer, the most paradigmatic, it would probably be Mozart. But if, in turn, one were to inquire about towering achievements carried out against insuperable odds, Beethoven would come to mind.

My purpose is to look at the great composers, primarily Mozart, secondarily Beethoven, and others as well. But not at the Mozart of the eighteenth century, a man who, we know from biographies, had a mind that worked with incredible speed, was a workaholic, was regarded in his time as a composer of music difficult to comprehend, had a volatile personality, and looked as far afield as he could for inspiration; and not the Beethoven of the early nineteenth century, a difficult man who wanted above all to get the recognition that was necessary for him to acquire the means to continue composing while facing enormous personal problems. We are discussing, instead, the Mozart and Beethoven of the present, as they are perceived by music lovers today, as living figures in today's musical culture. My purpose is not, however, to participate in the now widely respected study of reception history, but to characterize contemporary art music culture. The world of Western art music devotes itself to a large degree to composers long dead, music composed long ago, and performance practices developed in the distant past, and it evaluates its accomplishments in large measure by assessing its relationship with figures of the past, who, as a result, have a significant existence in the present.

The Pantheon

What are the ways in which the great composers rule the society of the Music Building, and what is it that Music Building society expresses by creating and maintaining the pantheon? Much of it has to do with the Music Building's view of its repertory as centered on a canon and the relationship of the canonic works to the images of the composers who created them. It is actually an ethnomusicological convention to ask this kind of question of other cultures, too.

Dreaming Songs

As a point of departure, I will begin with a brief excursion to the Blackfoot people of Montana and paraphrase a conversation I had with one of my Blackfoot teachers when doing fieldwork there. "This is my song," he said to me. "I dreamed this song myself." When do you sing it? I wanted to know. "It's part of the medicine pipe my uncle gave me," he replied, referring to a collection of sacred objects, each of which has its own song. The conversation turned on the nature of that medicine bundle and on the fact that, in the past at least, other Blackfoot medicine men had similar or identical bundles. And I discovered that my teacher's uncle had also dreamed a series of songs that went with this bundle. "But not that song," I prompted. "Yes, he dreamed that song too, and I heard him sing it later." "Well, how is it that this is now your song, that you dreamed it; after all, your uncle had already dreamed it. Is your song the same one, or different?" "To you, it's the same song. But to us, it might not be. If I dream it, it is a different song from when he dreams it." "You mean, the two of you sang that same song differently?" "No, I sing it just like my uncle. It's the dreaming that makes the difference." Music in Blackfoot culture is, on the one hand, its acoustic manifestation but, on the other, the act of creation, the dream or vision, in which a guardian spirit appears and teaches the dreamer a song. A song is importantly an act of creation that results from contact between human and supernatural.

Acts of Creation

In the Music Building, the act of creation is also central to the concept of the musical work.[1] Once, as I sat after dinner with a group of music scholars, I asked, "What if it were discovered that *Meistersinger* had not been composed by Wagner, but by Herr von X? Would it still be the same work?" "Certainly not," was the consensus, vehemently reinforced by an art historian (who had found himself in the circle) in reference to works by Leonardo or Van Gogh. The issue in the discussion was the identity of a work of art, and the question was whether in Western academic conception it was simply a physical object—a score or a painting—or whether the way it came about, the order in which its parts were added, the artist's intention, its relationship to the artist's other works and its cultural context in general, and the identity of the creator were also part of the work. In imagining a symphony written independently by two composers, my colleagues shared the view of my Blackfoot consultants and described the phenomenon as two separate works.

The person of creator and the authentication of the creation, its time and its place, are all of great importance to the members of Music Building society in their perception of their music. The most important feature of a piece is the identity of the composer, and recognizing the composer of what one hears or sees on the page is the surest way of proving membership in musical society. You turn on the radio and hear a piano, and the first thing you say to your music-loving companion is, "Oh, it's Chopin."

The quintessential importance of the relationship between a work of art and its creator is a major characteristic of Western classical music, literature, and art. It is this emphasis, for example, that has made the publication of the complete works of a composer, and of thematic catalogs that deal definitively with questions of attribution, so central to Western-style musicology. Perhaps a principal method for giving a composer the prestige one feels he or she deserves is to publish a thematic catalog. You must have one published if you are to be taken seriously as one of the biggies. It won't be surprising that this matter of authenticity and identity is particularly intense and has emotional overtones in the work of a small number of composers, the group called the great masters, the members of the pantheon.

In an article that analyzes the issues of musical attribution and its relationship to judgment, John Spitzer quotes two distinguished critics about Mozart's *Sinfonia Concertante*, K.297b.[2] Virgil Thomson, believing it to have been composed by Mozart, called it "tuneful, talented, fanciful, sound as an apple and as monumental as a palace courtyard"; Stanley Sadie—much later—said, "Ascribed to Mozart on the flimsiest evidence and never sounding remotely like a piece he would have put his name to, with its cheap and repetitive invention." Spitzer shows that those who thought it was Mozart's piece liked it, and those who didn't insisted that it couldn't be by Mozart. He couldn't have written such a bad piece; or, if Mozart did write it, it must be great and we're just not understanding it. Lots of other studies, and much anecdotal evidence, shows that an art music connoisseur's evaluation of a piece depends substantially on who wrote it. "What's that tiresome music?" you may ask. "But it's Schubert" is the reply, and you've been thoroughly put down.

Hearing and reading snippets that present Mozart and Schubert as deities beyond criticism supports the interpretation of the culture of Western art music in the contemporary world as a kind of religious system. Western art music lovers don't necessarily approach their music in a religious spirit, but they often say they are working in the service of music, an abstraction that exists without human intervention. One may say that music itself is the deity, as suggested by the commencement speaker who began by asserting that "what unites us is that we are all here in the service of music." But it is more instructive to look for the godlike in the pantheon of great masters who have scriptures (the manuscript, the authoritative, scholarly urtext edition reflecting the earliest sources, and the authentic performance); who are served by a priesthood of performers and musicologists; who are celebrated in and surrounded by rituals such as concert, rehearsal, lesson, and practice session; and who are commemorated by controversies regarding the authenticity of manuscripts, letters, and portraits. Some scholars with an interest in the belongings, instruments, and portraits of great composers refer to these as the "sacred relics" of music history.[3] The need to perform the works of composers as *they* would have wished to hear them (not so much as they might actually have heard them) and the insistence that one identify the greatness in these works, avoiding the usual critical treatment applied to ordinary artists, are evidence of this sacredness.

Like the ancient Greek, Germanic, and West African pantheons, the group of great composers has a society of their own, relates to each other like members of a family, and plays roles in dramas. The priesthood of performers and scholars devote much energy to the study of their interrelationships, such as the concept of composers writing music, as it were, "about each other," with quotations, variations, dedications, and parody; the measurement of similarities and differences among composers' styles; who influences whom and who was ahead of whom in the evolution of styles and genres; the composers' knowledge of each others' music; and more. The humans who maintain their music associate themselves with the deities in various ways, manipulate them and their works, are impressed by both relationships and contrasts, and do much to approximate themselves to divine status by striving to emulate the deities.

Names in Stone

The nature of the pantheon is clearly articulated, for example, in the engravings of names on music school buildings and concert halls. Despite changing tastes and occasional idiosyncrasies of architects and philanthropists, the pantheon has a few chief gods, a consistent entourage, and the occasional upstart whose cult becomes prominent enough to elevate him to the appropriate level. At the University of Illinois at Urbana-Champaign, Smith Music Hall (built in the 1920s) bears only four names: Bach, Beethoven, Haydn, and Palestrina. At Indiana University in Bloomington, in a building of the late 1930s, a much more extended version appears. Along the front, the most prominent; on the sides, a presumably lesser group:

Wagner, Haydn, Bach, Mozart, Beethoven

Mendelssohn	Verdi
Schumann	Handel
Brahms	Sibelius
Schubert	Liszt
Saint-Saens	Chopin

Inside the Recital Hall, on the left and right walls, names of composers are likewise inscribed:

Mozart	Beethoven
Mendelssohn	Wagner
Liszt	Chopin

All overlap, but the arrangements differ. On the outside of the building at Indiana, the structure seems to reflect greatness or significance. Not many would argue with Bach's front-and-center position, although some might disagree with Wagner's prominent spot. But that

such a distinction (and obviously it is there, between absolute greatness and a slightly lower lever) should have been made by the designer in Bloomington seems significant. Inside, however, the deities have more specific roles. The traditional Mozart-Beethoven
duality is in front, as they face each other next to the stage, the supreme human and the "man loved by God." There is the dramatic
contrast—as perceived in the twentieth century—between Wagner
and Mendelssohn, as the heavy, totally German, sometime anti-Semite
master of the longest works faces the Jew who traveled widely and
sought influence from abroad, who seemed (so his music sounds) not
to have taken himself all that seriously and wrote short works. But
as the pantheon is dominated by Germans, it still, as each example
shows, grudgingly admits a few outsiders, as Liszt and Chopin, Hungarian and Pole, masters of the piano, follow the masters of orchestra and opera.

At Harvard University, inside the auditorium of Paine Hall (outside the Heartland to be sure but perhaps reflecting the same values),
the names are arranged thus:

Handel, Bach, Haydn, Mozart, Beethoven, Schubert, Chopin, Wagner, Schumann

Gluck	Mendelssohn
Rameau	Weber
Couperin	Berlioz
Tartini	Liszt
Scarlatti	Verdi
Monteverde	Grieg
Palestrina	Tschaikowsky
Lasso	Franck
	Brahms

In front are the great Germans (plus Chopin), with lesser figures
on the sides. Furthermore, there is an approximately chronological
sequence from left to right, as if to remind us that there is history,
and its high point is not at the culminating end, nor at the beginning (after which all went downhill), but in the center of the time

line. The hierarchy is reflected in a bell-shaped curve of history.[4] By contrast, a building once housing a music school in Northampton, Massachusetts, has only two names on its front: Mozart and Handel.

Extracting values or principles from these engravings (and from other groupings found at a few other academic institutions in the United States as well as on several concert halls in such cities as Boston, New York, and Dallas—and many in Europe) would be a bit like constructing the dinosaur from one tail bone. Were the inclusion and the placement of particular composers intentional, and do they follow well-established patterns? Is all this a component of culture in the sense that it is accepted by many individuals in the society, or is it idiosyncrasy? I am inclined to think, but can only guess, that in each case the architect or designer, or the university in its role of educator of students and the public, must have listed the names on these various buildings, and decided their order, for a purpose.

One purpose may be to exhibit the consistency of the culture's musical values. Tastes may change, Rossini may someday become more popular and highly regarded than Tschaikowsky, but the eternal value of the group on the front of the Indiana and Harvard buildings is not questioned. It seems unlikely that the array of names is intended merely as a monument to the taste of the time in which the building was constructed. The institutions seem, rather, to be saying that what is played in the Music Building and in the Recital Hall may be greatly varied, but the audience must remember that certain figures—the pantheon—dominate permanently.

Moreover, the names may be there, high on the music buildings as a statement to the common people, the philistines and peasants who walk by. The buildings seem to be shouting these hallowed names with defiance because they fear perhaps not to be taken seriously, devoted as they are to a subject once relegated to women's schools, the music of ridiculous, long-haired composers, the bewigged Mozart and the madly pacing Beethoven.

The names in stone also constitute an act of worship and edification. Students who walk by music buildings should be constantly reminded whose music should be respected most. However, when I asked a class of thirty-five music majors at the University of Illinois to name the four composers on Smith Music Hall, only one knew any, and most were unaware of the engravings. In mitigation, the names are placed quite high on the building, almost as if the intention were to keep them out of sight.

Engraving the names of artists, philosophers, and scientists is common on academic buildings, libraries, and theaters. It began in nineteenth-century Europe but seems to have developed more in the United States, appropriate perhaps in a culture in which people often wear their principles on their sleeves—or rather, on their bumper stickers and T-shirts. It may be significant, however, that there is more engraving on university music buildings than on buildings in which other disciplines, other fields, are taught, and significant as well that a tendency to delete the names (as on the outside of Boston's Symphony Hall) has arisen in the last few decades.

In the world of classical music, the act of creation, the person of the music's creator, are the most important things that happen in addition to the existence of a canon. The Music Building in Bloomington is indeed primarily for Wagner, Haydn, Bach, and the rest. Many things that go on in the building may change, but this primary commitment is unalterable. And yet, when the center of musical taste changes and it becomes almost embarrassing to list composers once much more esteemed than today (Ambroise Thomas, Christoph Willibald Gluck, and Orlando di Lasso come to mind), when tastes change radically and the musical world seems to cry out, "We were wrong," the names on certain buildings are replaced by blank shields.

The names under the roofs mark the buildings as shrines, reminding music lovers of their primary duty, homage to the great masters, as the music buildings are shrines to them and them alone—for musicians and music lovers do worship the composers. Their busts stand on pianos; the instruments they owned are icons; and the watches, eyeglasses, and fans they owned command exorbitant prices at auctions.[5] The authentication of locks of hair and pieces of bone is almost as significant as the authentication of musical works.[6]

A Roundtable of Deities

To follow the analogy of pantheons a bit further, in the society of the Music Building, musical life is built on a group of widely articulated beliefs, mainly about composers, and these have something (but not necessarily much) to do with historical reality. There is Mozart, the composer of sweetness, who was such a genius that he didn't have to try but who died young and is seen even by those not engaged in my idiosyncratic kind of analysis as somehow divine. It's a view that has also been expressed by biographers such as Wolfgang Hildesheimer, who describes Mozart as "the greatest genius in recorded human history,"

and Alfred Einstein, who sees him as the single truly universal composer.[7] Rossini has been quoted (probably apocryphally) as saying that
"Beethoven is the greatest composer, but Mozart is the only one."[8]
Nicolas Slonimsky identifies Mozart as the "supreme genius of music,"
whereas Beethoven is (merely) "the great German composer who represents the fullest maturity of the allied classical forms of the sonata,
concerto, string quartet and the symphony."[9]

Mozart represents the concept of genius who accomplishes without effort; Beethoven—also a genius, of course—nevertheless symbolizes great human achievement requiring enormous effort. They
are two sides of the coin that pervades the culture of the Music Building, symbolizing an important duality and also a set of oppositions
in twentieth-century Western thought—genius and labor, the light
and the heavy, sweetness and salt, and also divine and human, Zeus
and Prometheus.

The contrast of Mozart and Beethoven may be the central paradigm of musical thought in the art music world of Heartland U. But
other composers also have unique personalities, much like gods, although the literature about them, respectful and appreciative, does
not usually place them in the same league with Beethoven and
Mozart. It is tempting to go through the list of great masters to see
how each is seen as musician and person, but I must be content with
two brief examples, Wagner and Haydn.

Richard Wagner emerges as an evil deity whose musical ability—
that is, his supernatural power—is unquestioned although sometimes
used to accomplish evil. His image is one of disdain for other humans, of overpowering nationalism, disregard for personal loyalty, and
political and social instability. Associated with negative forces—German nationalism, the eventual rise of Nazism, and anti-Semitism—
he is admired but disliked by some, for his music in its sound and
social and historical context deals with issues of the musical world.
The rather obvious subtext of his opera *Meistersinger* is, after all, a
critique of the structure of musical life and values of Wagner's own
time. Recognized as a grand innovator, the man who had the last
word in the age of functional harmony, possibly suspect precisely
because he did not keep art and life sufficiently separate, he is a kind
of musical Shiva, destroyer and creator together, or Loge the magi-
cian, the clever but unpredictable god of fire from his own *Ring*.

Of quite opposite image, Joseph Haydn is perceived as a modest, obedient person, called "Papa" in part because of his innovations but more perhaps because of his caring nature. Despite his role as the developer of much that dominated through the nineteenth century, musicians do not speak of him with awe as the man who made things happen. Rather, the musical public thinks of his music as competent, pleasant, interesting, but rarely as moving or stirring. In the composers' roundtable, he has the position of a helper, the one who taught Beethoven and early on recognized the great genius of Mozart. Not a flamboyant figure, his role among the deities is relatively colorless, a kind of Apollo, the predictable nice guy of the Greek pantheon.

The perception of a special relationship of the images of Beethoven and Schubert goes back virtually to their own time and was emphasized by George Grove, author of their major biographies in the earliest editions of *Grove's Dictionary*.[10] Beethoven the hard and tough, the complex, intellectual, motivic, and, in the end, masculine (and thus the representative of human artifice, of culture) contrasts with Schubert the gentle and soft, the simple and straightforward, emotional, melodic, and, as one might expect, feminine (and thus closer to nature). That these adjectives probably do little to explain the working methods of these composers or the perceptions of their immediate audiences is beside the point for this discussion. The labels continue to play a role in musical thinking and writing.[11]

Tying the differences between Beethoven and Schubert to contrastive sexual orientation is a way of working the musically important differences between them into strands of thought significant in the 1980s.[12] But in the end, the insistence that Beethoven and Schubert (who, objectively, in a context of the music of the world would come up looking very much alike) represent opposite ends of some kind of continuum may actually come from the desire in our culture to look at music as an essentially dualistic phenomenon and from our tendency to think of the world of art music as one ruled by a group of deities, each of whom has a distinct musical and biographical image.

In the musical culture of the midwestern School of Music, these deities interact in complex ways. Scholars analyze and emphasize different composers' repeated use of certain motifs or techniques as either "borrowings" or "commentaries" on each other.[13] In textbooks, program notes, and conversations of musicians, composers may be discussed in reference to each other, as individuals related to the group. Elementary texts also make much of personal associations—Haydn's praise of Mozart and his acquaintance with Beethoven, Schubert's statements at Beethoven's grave, and the friendship of Schumann and Brahms. It would seem that these associations give legitimacy to the pantheon.

The idea of mythological, divine, royal extended family or closely knit group, each member with specific function, has always been significant in European symbolic thought. Aside from the Greek, Roman, and Germanic pantheons, there is the Arthurian roundtable (with a collection of heroes similar to those of Homeric and South Slavic epics), cabinet of government ministers, the American Constitutional Convention of Revolutionary heroes, and, for that matter, the musicians' guild in Wagner's *Die Meistersinger von Nürnberg* and the group of medieval singers in his *Tannhäuser*. The master composers too are seen as figures who fill roles in a small society and interrelate fictionally through their personalities and objectively through their music.

Agents of the Supernatural?

The Greek pantheon, we are told, consisted of some permanent and dominant members—Zeus, Ares, Poseidon, and Aphrodite—and others whose popularity came and went, or whose divinity was only partial. Cults developed around some deities for certain periods, and others were associated with particular localities. The classic sociological study of symphony orchestra repertory by John Mueller suggests that the pantheon of composers has had a similar kind of existence.[14] Dealing only with American symphony orchestras and audiences to 1945, Mueller shows that the American symphony repertory was dominated by four composers—Beethoven, Brahms, Tchaikovsky, and (a distant fourth) Mozart. The history of the repertory to about 1950 also is comprised of a group of composers who maintained a steady but low profile in the repertory, some who were in an ascending phase of attention (Bruckner and Mahler), others in a descending phase (Schubert and Mendelssohn), and a few whose life-cycles seemed to have been completed and are barely known today.

There are various reasons for the differential treatment of these composers. Kingsbury describes the importance of the concepts of talent and genius—gifts from above, not something you can acquire—in the culture of the Music Building.[15] The great masters are geniuses; others have talent or merely worked hard. What then of the composers who don't make the circle of deities? The rhetoric of American academic music lovers takes for granted a sharp distinction between great masters and others, using the definition given above. Discussion of music usually focuses on the masters and creates a universe for them in which certain ones are supreme and others totally unacceptable, but unacceptable only within this "great master" circle. Characteristically, a few composers are singled out for special praise, likely Beethoven, Mozart, Bach, and Schubert. Some may be the subject of harsh criticism—most typically Wagner, Brahms, Mahler, Bruckner, Schumann, and Handel—for reasons such as the excessive length of their pieces, the excessive emotional content of their style, or pretentiousness, pomposity, and redundancy. If, however, the conversation were to turn to "minor" composers such as Jan Vaclav Tomášek and Jan Hugo Voříšek, Czech contemporaries of Schubert's, or Mozart's contemporaries Giovanni Paisiello and the antihero of *Amadeus,* Antonio Salieri, the flavor is often patronizing, and it would be taken for granted that one is now in a different league.[16] Lavish praise for Paisiello never suggests that he is superior to Wagner, whom the speaker may just have savaged. We (in the Music Building) can distinguish major leagues from bush leagues, never fear, and our rhetoric takes these concepts for granted. In music school rhetoric, the term *genius* is ordinarily reserved for deceased artists, whereas the living are more frequently said to have "talent."

It is interesting to see that the pantheon consists largely of ethnic Germans and that this does not make much difference to the musicians or audiences. Perhaps it is just taken for granted. But the contrast with art museums, in which artists are normally identified by nation (even when hardly necessary, as in the case of Leonardo or Michelangelo), suggests a difference. Mozart, Beethoven, Bach, and the rest are in a sense supranational (as far as American audiences are concerned); when you become a musical deity, you may lose your nationality.

This basically secular society seeks culture heroes, originators of the society's central treasures, and surrounds them with the concepts and paraphernalia once specific to religion itself. The great composers, through their genius, mysteriously created the great music. They are not seen as ordinary humans who accomplished something and died, but as living beings still. Thus, teachers occasionally refer to the presumed desires of a composer by saying such things as, "Here is how

Bach wants this," and, "This really sounds like Chopin playing." In the concept of living masters there is a confluence of worship and historicism—perhaps two opposite sides of a coin. We wish to play Mozart as he would wish us to play his music—although it is questionable that he had such precise ideas at all—and we want to reconstruct the sound, the environment, perhaps even aspects of the cultural context, of Mozart's own performances.[17] As music historians, we want to know precisely how it was done; as worshipful musicians, we also want to carry it out that way. The two attitudes may not produce the same sound, and the annals of music history and criticism are replete with debates as to the need to play Mozart (and the other masters) in the way their music sounded in their day or as they might wish it to sound today, judging performances from their lofty engraved perches above the third-floor windows.[18]

Special acts of worship, such as the celebration of anniversaries, placing names on buildings and busts on pianos, lavishing attention on composers' homes, possessions, and, most of all, manuscripts—the sacred texts—suggest behavior derived from the customs of various religious systems. That Mozart—and the others—are in a sense living deities is illustrated by debates among scholars and musicians on the merits of performing all of his works at New York's Lincoln Center in 1991, debates in which this ritual would "help" Mozart.[19] Viewing our musical culture as an analogue to religion can provide insights into the mind of art music society. But the classical system is not the only music in American culture susceptible to this kind of analysis—take Elvis Presley for a start.

Mythological Variations

The Myth of Beaver

In the work of some anthropologists and ethnomusicologists it is suggested that the culture of a society—the vast number of things and ideas of which a culture consists—can be encapsulated in a single statement, for example, in a type of performance or in a myth.[20] If the great masters are, in a way, the deities of the belief system of our art music culture, one might expect them to be the subject of a mythology that explains this culture. Could we find the quintessence of our ideas about art music in a kind of mythic duel between Mozart and Beethoven replicated at other levels? To show what I have in mind, it is necessary to summarize an important myth of the Black-foot people because it seems to me to explain the principal Black-foot ideas about music.[21]

The story concerns the interaction of a human family and the supernatural figure of beaver (perceived perhaps as partially human and thus more appropriately called "beaverman"), who has a role of a kind of lord of the part of the world below the surface of water.[22] A great human hunter has killed a specimen of each animal and bird, and their dressed skins decorate his tent. While he is hunting, the beaver comes to visit his wife and seduces her, and she follows him into the water. After four days she returns to her husband, and in time gives birth to a beaver child. Affairs were unforgivable in Blackfoot society, but the hunter continues to be kind to his wife and the child. The beaver, visiting, expresses pleasure at this and offers to give the hunter some of his supernatural power as a reward. They smoke to-gether, and then the beaverman begins to sing many songs, each containing a request for a particular bird or animal skin. The hunter gives the skins, one by one, and receives, in return, the songs of the beaver and the supernatural power that goes with them, and thus the principal Blackfoot ritual.

This myth imparts some important things about Blackfoot mu-sic: It comes from the supernatural, songs come as whole units, you learn them in one hearing, and they are objects that can be traded for physical objects. The musical system reflects the cultural system, as each being in the environment has its song. Music reflects and contains supernatural power. It's something that only men use and perform, but women are instrumental in bringing about its existence. Music is given to humans who act morally, gently, and in a civilized manner. It has specific roles and functions and is used in a prescribed ritual. It comes about as the result of a period of dwelling with the supernatural, after which a major aspect of culture is brought, so, in a way, it symbolizes humanity and Blackfootness.

Myths of Mozart

The mythology of the Music Building has more characters, and facts and fancy are intertwined in its stories. Yet these stories are also myths in the sense that they explain complex reality in capsule form to the ignorant and the young. Let us look for Mozart mythology.

The kinds of themes most widely touched on in biography and program notes, most widely believed by the general music-loving public, most frequently told to children in their music lessons, might have that function.[23]

We have a young boy with incredible talent and ability; no one could really explain his feats. His father took him to show him off for the royalty of Europe, but he seemed not to appreciate these advantages and eventually got along badly with his father. Later on, he tried to make his living as a composer but was always poor. He was not appreciated in his own city of Salzburg and also not very much in Vienna; only in the somewhat foreign Prague was he understood, and from his childhood on he was always on the go. Most important, perhaps, is the belief that Mozart could compose without trying, that his music came full-blown into his mind and had only to be written down. He could hear a piece of music and play it back unerringly by ear, and he was a superb improviser. His musical style remained essentially unchanged throughout his life. He was hated by his rival Salieri and died very young, a mysterious death. When terminally ill, he was asked to write a requiem and had the idea that it was for himself, but he died before he could finish it. His accomplishments were the result of some kind of supernatural power, thus the great attention to his mysterious death. But there was something childlike about him, and he was impractical in worldly matters. The main point was that he was *born* a genius, an essentially European notion related in earlier times to social immobility and the belief in elites. Except at moments such as a bicentennial, Mozart is held in even higher esteem in Europe than in North America, as his kind of persona fits better the older European notion of how art and life relate. In their lessons, children are told about Mozart first; he is thought to be a composer whom a child could understand, a man who composed when he was a child and whose childlike nature never quite left him.

And of Beethoven

In my description of conventional wisdom, Mozart is typically compared and contrasted with a composer whose music is better for older people: Beethoven, a different kind of person and, like his music, difficult, hard to get along with—in various ways quite the opposite of Mozart. As Mozart's death was mysterious, so were the dates of

Beethoven's birth and his descent. He had a dark and brooding look, suffered greatly, was frequently disappointed, never found the right woman, and there was the tragedy of his deafness. His music didn't come easily; you could tell he had to work hard to write it, you had to work hard to listen to it. It changed throughout his life, his early works are extremely different from his late ones. He had no children, but a nephew on whom he doted yet who disappointed him. He had a hard life; his deafness dominates our idea of him; he labored, sketched his works for years before getting them right; and he is seen as a rebel and a struggler against many kinds of bonds. The apocryphal story of his meeting with Goethe at Teplitz (where he upbraided Goethe for showing excessive respect to the emperor) is indicative. He took his artistic responsibilities seriously, giving up much for the spiritual aspects of his music. A genius like Mozart, he had to work hard to become and be one. It is perhaps no coincidence that he has been, to Americans, the quintessential great master of music. This is, after all, the culture in which hard work was once prized above all and labor rewarded; you weren't born to greatness, but were supposed to struggle to achieve it.

We know that the historical figures of Mozart and Beethoven weren't all that different in their attitudes toward music and their work habits, that Mozart was a workaholic, something of a rebel, did some sketching, and was regarded as a difficult composer in his lifetime, whereas Beethoven had a full life that included much beyond his work as a composer. The point is that in looking at the popular conceptions of musicians and music lovers, ferreting out myths from various sources, we can learn about the relationship of the musical system to the rest of culture. The two composers represent opposite values; they are the opposites of a Lévi-Straussian diagram. They are also paradigms, in the field of music, of our tendency to look at the world as sets of opposites.

As the Blackfoot beaver myth shows us important ideas about the way the Blackfoot people conceive of their songs, our ideas about Mozart and Beethoven reveal some of our values. For example, there is conflict between inspiration and labor. There is the tendency of genius to suffer. The great composer has supernatural connections and may be a stranger. Music is mysterious; its great practitioners come, in some sense, from outside the culture—a characteristic of the Western attitude toward music discussed in many sorts of musical literature. The composers are the main units of musical thought and recognition. Their configuration illuminates such major structural principles of Western music and society as hierarchy and duality, stability and progress.

Pairs, Sweets, and Oranges: A Scherzo

We can find evidence of the importance of dualism as a core value of the Western art music world in many corners of musical life, from the centrality of the Mozart-Beethoven paradigm to the significance of musical forms such as the sonata even in today's society in which duality is the driving force and on to the opposition of concepts such as human accomplishment and supernatural inspiration, of labor and genius. Musical dualism even attacks us, it seems, when we are waving our arms to beautiful records in the privacy of our homes, or reading science fiction, or eating our desserts.

The Benefits of Duality

Musicians in Madras used to say to me, an American, "We have our trinity of great composers, Tyagaraja, Syama Sastri, and Dikshitar, just as you have your trinity," meaning Haydn, Mozart, and Beethoven. The number *3* is important in our culture, but dualism actually plays a greater role in the conceptual framework of the culture of Western art music.

Let me illustrate with a bit of trivia from the history of musicology, a 1928 work about the character of rhythm by Gustav Becking, a now obscure German musicologist who died in 1945 and who may be considered a precursor of American ethnomusicologists interested in culture types.[24] His book promulgates the theory that one could intuitively understand and classify pieces, composers, styles, and periods by using a typology of rhythmic flow known as the "Becking curves." Two principal categories are named for their exemplars, Mozart and Beethoven, and, although a third miscellaneous category is built around Bach, Becking clearly prefers the bipolar structure. He sees the classical music system as essentially an opposition between monistic and dualistic, spiritualist and materialist, idealist and naturalist.

Becking may just have been idiosyncratic, but in many ways our art music culture divides the world into sets of pairs. There is the major-minor dyad, perhaps the first bit of music theory learned by fledgling piano students. The significance of binary forms and their derivatives as bases for the quintessential genres of the Classical and Romantic periods; the contrast between the two main themes of sonata form; the importance of sonata form, whose main character-istic is the presentation of opposites; the contrast between aria and recitative—all this underscores the driving force of dualism in the music most standard in today's art music world. Musicians and stu-dents are readily if not always accurately oriented to composers by pairs: Leonin-Perotin, Ockeghem-Obrecht, Peri-Caccini, Cesti-Cav-alli, Handel-Bach, Haydn-Mozart, Schumann-Mendelssohn, Berlioz-Liszt, Donizetti-Bellini, Verdi-Wagner (but also Wagner-Brahms), Smetana-Dvořák, Bruckner-Mahler, Bartók-Kodály, Schoenberg-Stravinsky, many partaking of some of the kinds of contrast that the Mozart-Beethoven paradigm presents.[25]

A Matter of Synesthesia

Some readers may perceive the preceding paragraphs as the scherzo of this chapter and will see the next section, which moves us into a phase of ethnomusicology not well developed, as its trio. In his in-fluential book *The Anthropology of Music,* Alan Merriam suggests that one can learn about the arts in culture through the study of synes-thesia, "the experience of an associated sensation when another sense is stimulated."[26] In other words, seeing certain works of art might remind you of a particular odor and hearing certain kinds of music might make you see particular color combinations or give you a sen-sation of taste.

Mozart seems to me to be widely regarded as "the sweet compos-er." The childlikeness associated with him may play a role, but my main evidence concerns his association with sweet foods. In a classic Viennese cookbook by Alice Urbach, the name of Mozart appears with some prominence; there are two kinds of tarts (*Krapfen*) with chocolate, marzipan, and pistachios. By now, too, virtually everyone has been exposed to a delicious kind of candy, *Mozartkugeln* (Mozart balls).[27] A couple of afternoons in the telephone directory section of the local public library yields five sweet shops named for Mozart in North America—in New York, Washington, San Francisco, Toronto, Vancou-ver. (Mozart cafes abound in Germany and Austria.) There are liqueurs named for Mozart, for his famous sister and fellow-musician Nannerl, and for his most popular work, "Eine kleine Nachtmusik"; there is also a sweet California wine named Mozart. To be sure, even before the 1991 bicentennial there had developed a kind of Mozart industry, and perhaps it has nothing to do with musical culture and its values. Significantly, however, it has not penetrated salty foods, cheeses, or meat-and-potato restaurants. There are, on the other hand, no sweets named for Beethoven, whose name in North America is given only to a restaurant in San Francisco and, symbol of the hard-laboring musician, the Beethoven Piano Moving Company in New York.

Connecting types of music with emotions, odors, colors, and tastes is a widespread phenomenon in world music. The association of ragas with characteristics such as devotion, joy, calm, fatigue, flirtation, and heaviness; of Persian *dastgahs* with warlikeness, majesty, sorrow, and even saltiness, is well known.[28] The association of Mozart with lightness and sweetness and of Beethoven with difficulty and perhaps even salt is an analogue. Indeed, in our map of Western classical music, the composers are perhaps the analogue of the modes of South and West Asia. After all, if you ask an Indian musician to tell you of what his music consists, he will probably say, "Why the ragas, of course." And an American classical musician? Perhaps she would say, "The great composers, of course, like Beethoven, Bach, Mozart."

To return to Urbach's classic cookbook, whose specialty seems to be its recipes for sweets: Why no entry for Beethoven, none for Haydn, also none for other great musical residents of Vienna such as Schoenberg, Brahms, and the various Strausses? And why, for that matter, if there is a Mozart industry centered on the sweets of his birthplace of Salzburg is there no equivalent industry centered on the salty, the spicy, and the culinarily complex emanating from Bonn, city of Beethoven's birth, and none for Haydn (concentrating perhaps on "sensible" food?) coming out of that master's city of extended residence, Eisenstadt?[29] Is it the particularly apt association of the sweet with the apparently easy?

Whatever the answer, many music lovers see Mozart as the "seamless composer" because no one else pursues quite the same logic in moving musically from one thing to the next, always with what appears to be perfect ease and complete absence of effort or laboriousness. The homology of effortless and sweet is clear in our metaphors. It is sweets, and particularly chocolate, that "go down easily" and provide no obstacles, and Mozart's music is easy, flows naturally, and moves without obstacle because it is by a composer who, it appears, wrote easily and didn't have to labor. To Mozart, people now often think, composing was "like taking candy from a baby," or "easy as pie," or perhaps "a piece of cake."

It is instructive to note a second composer whose music fits this model: Franz Schubert, represented in Urbach's cookbook by *Schubert-krapfen* (Schubert tarts), named for the artist who, the legend tells us, loved eating and drinking and is said to have composed, so full of ideas was he, on the back of a menu while waiting to be served. (Or does this inform us more about the efficiency of Viennese waiters in 1820?) But for Mozart, it is the personality myth supported by the "sweetness" of the music that permits us today to make him the subject of lighthearted yet admiring parody, such as P.D.Q. Bach/Peter Schickele's *A Little Nightmare Music* and *Stoned Guest* and, indirectly, in the inexplicable title of Stephen Sondheim's waltz-dominated *A Little Night Music*. Mozart did it to himself in his "Musical Joke," in his scatological canons, by wryly quoting himself and others in *Don Giovanni,* while Beethoven seemed generally to be much more serious and mostly avoided making fun of himself in his music.

The Gift of the Otherworldly

Mozart and Beethoven play roles in many works of literature, drama, and popular culture, and their representations have been subjected to detailed analysis. For a sample of the polarity in literary work, however, consider Anthony Burgess, the novelist and occasional composer. Alex, the despicable protagonist of *A Clockwork Orange,* has a curious side to him—his love of classical music, particularly of "Ludwig van," as he names the composer, who at times thunders through the book (and through Stanley Kubrick's film) with his Ninth Symphony. At the end of another novel of Burgess's, *The End of the World News,* fifty survivors of a planetary collision zoom into the future in a spaceship to the sound of Mozart's C-major "Jupiter Symphony" no. 41.[30] Many music lovers, if asked to identify Beethoven's most valuable work, would name the Ninth Symphony, and Burgess and Kubrick use it to symbolize the values of Western culture, which in the plot of *A Clockwork Orange* are in jeopardy. In certain ways, it is also Beethoven's biggest work. Burgess presents the "Jupiter," Mozart's largest symphonic effort, literally as the final climax of the world's music. To Burgess, as to many, Beethoven is the peak of worldly achievement, and Mozart the gift of the otherworldly.

Orchestral Episodes

A major theme of ethnomusicological discourse is that fundamental values of a culture are expressed in its music. The literature gives abundant examples, but I can refer, for an introduction, to two of my own field experiences. In Iran, the classical music system was re-created in the decades before and after about 1900 in a form compatible and competitive with, but in some ways similar to, Western classical music.[31] The importance of improvisatory behavior and the value of individualism and of surprising people in Iranian social life become readily apparent in the improvisations in Persian classical music and in their centrality within the entire musical system.[32]

It stands to reason that a musical system like this, even if not understood thoroughly by many Iranians, could detail certain values that were important to the culture at large: hierarchy, guidance provided directly from a central authority and balanced by the importance of human equality in Islam, individualism and the associated values of surprise and unpredictability, and the importance of introductory behavior in formal events. One can identify the social values by the ubiquity of certain behavior patterns, the character of works of art that are greatly admired and idealized, and the structure of society as it is presented in anthropological literature. Analysis of the music itself and commentary on what is essential about it from musicians provide the musical counterpart. Asking the same kind of question of Native Americans Plains culture, I found that the importance of the concept of the heroic in Blackfoot culture is expressed in the heroic sound of the music and in the risks one undergoes to acquire music.[33]

For Western art music culture, the available illustrations are legion, and I will touch on a few very briefly, eschewing greater detail or discussion of the validity of the methodology.[34] The principal question is whether the *large* performances in the Music Building of *great* works by *great* composers and the *largest* ensemble—the symphony orchestra—further explain the importance of the great master concept for insiders as well as the Martian observer. The question can be illuminated by comments on the taxonomy of music as revealed by costume; on the orchestra as metaphor of factory, political organization, and colonial empire; and on the role of the great composers such as Mozart in concert programs.

Clothes Make the Musician

The E.T. discovers that people wear different kinds of clothes when publicly playing (or hearing) different kinds of music, and that one good way to know what kinds of music the society of the Music Building thinks exist is to track costuming. The relative status of repertoires and genres, and musical events, is expressed, among other things, in the dress or costume of performers and even of the audience. The correlation between costume and musical category is so strong that a hearing-impaired person could usually identify style and category by noting whether the musicians wear tuxedos, blazers, turtlenecks, robes, dhotis, Elizabethan garb, T-shirts with holes, or leather jackets. All of this will be familiar to American readers, but recalling it helps us see the boundaries and hierarchies in our musical taxonomy (chapters 3 and 4).

The need to wear a uniform is in itself worthy of contemplation. A uniform accomplishes the depersonalization of the individual, giving the orchestra a faceless quality that is exacerbated by requirements of such uniform behavior as bowing. The audience is expected to think of the orchestra as a unit, an organism with a personality that transcends that of the individual musician. Uniforms also suggest cultural and social roles. Your uniform tells people what you do, and musical uniforms tell what kind of music musicians "do." And so the uniforms of various kinds of musicians impart important insights about the taxonomy of music. They identify and separate the classes of music—classical, rock, country, experimental, and early—and also associate them with other aspects of the culture. Thus, choir robes suggest the importance of sacred music in choral repertories. Band uniforms provide evidence of the military association. The idiosyncratic dress of rock musicians reminds us of the dissident aspects of rock music. It is indicative of gender roles in American society that these uniforms derive principally from men's dress, that there is less difference among their various female versions, and that women sometimes simply use the men's versions of uniforms. Musicians' clothes symbolize the ways in which the musical system subdivides itself; they also integrate the domain of music into culture as a whole.

The tendency of musicians in Western culture to wear clothes different from their everyday attire contrasts with the custom of Plains Indian powwow singers, who wear precisely and determinedly what they might wear at other times—jeans, T-shirts, and farmer's caps—despite the clearly special nature of musical performance. Perhaps they do so because virtually all others present—the dancers—are in costume, and the singers wish to separate themselves from them. Although this explanation may seem at best moderately convincing, the fact remains that powwow singers want to look different from the dancers, who are their principal audience.

Reflection of Structures

The units of music-making the world over are comprised of individuals, but in many societies they combine into standardized ensembles that assume identities and personalities of their own. Nowhere is this more important than in Western classical music, where one speaks readily of the Budapest Quartet, the Chicago Symphony, and the Mormon Tabernacle Choir, usually without knowing the names of any of the members. The impersonal existence of ensembles as units seems to be related to the concepts essential to an industrial culture, and the symphony orchestra is the centerpiece.[35]

In the history of Western music, the standardization, maturity, and eventual expansion of the symphony orchestra, as well as its internal organization, correlate with the development of European industrialization and the development of similarly artificial persons, the corporations of business and industry. The symphony orchestra of Haydn and Mozart coincides with the beginning of factories. As the industrial system grew, the orchestra also expanded from the late eighteenth century into the twentieth, first typically adding clarinets, then trombones, tubas, and piccolo, English horn, bass clarinet, saxophone, euphonium, piano, organ, a vast array of percussion, and divided string sections. The practice of unison bowing was added, and other kinds of uniformity under a time-beating conductor who was not also playing keyboard or first violin.

A hierarchical substructure developed; the third-desk violist is supposed to be better than the musician sitting behind him or her, or to have more seniority. The first-chair performers of the sections are department heads of a sort. And the concert master, whose main visible role is to preside over the ceremonial tuning up of the orchestra (actually led by the first oboe), is a kind of factory foreman keeping things in shape for the management. There is also the matter of specialization in scoring, a growing practice until about 1890–1910, when huge orchestras were used but all or most instruments played together only a tiny percentage of the time. Note the labor-management relationship of conductor and orchestra, with management being relatively invulnerable except to revolution. These parallels could be carried to interesting lengths, but there are many ways to interpret them. Yet it is attractive to think of the orchestra as a kind of factory for making music, gradually adopting the refinements and efficiencies developed in the industrial world.

A further parallel comes from the colonialist counterpart of the industrial revolution—the plantation workers of the orchestra directed by a native headman for the foreign management, related perhaps to the widespread employment of foreign conductors in late nineteenth and early twentieth centuries. The orchestra is also a kind of army and reflects a structure found in the military domain of culture that closely reflects important parts of the Western social structure. The conductor is the general, the "baton" of military origin.[36] The conductor gets credit for victories, is listed on the album cover, takes bows, but is not heard and so risks little. (The enlisted "troops" tell jokes: "Have you ever heard a conductor's baton play out of tune?") The occupants of the first chairs are officers who have a certain amount of authority over their troops, whose main task is to march— that is, bow and finger—in unison, mainly for the appearance of discipline. There is little democratic discussion. The conductor decides on tempo, one does not vote; at most, the orchestra may rebel and remove the conductor. Actually, there is rarely much hope of that because the orchestra may be an army of mercenaries whose conductor can barely speak their language and has little sympathy for their culture. The conductor may be comparable to many eighteenth- and nineteenth-century generals (who throughout the world were often Germans) and is the most successful illustration of the Western tradition of musician as cultural or even racial outsider. Conductors are often permitted or even expected to be eccentric; sport long hair, strange dress, and a foreign accent; and lead a strange life. It is a pattern that, despite the vast degree of culture change in the Western world's last several centuries, continues to maintain itself.

Notation, the Universal Language

In American and European society, the concept of literacy is a metaphor for knowing a culture or a cultural domain. In recent years, this metaphor has even led to curious juxtapositions, such as the concept of someone who is "television-literate" as one who knows how to divine the central message of television without reading. "Cultural literacy" became a code word for knowing and understanding a central canon, and one might expect the concept of "musical literacy" to suggest understanding of the musical masterworks of Bach, Mozart, and Beethoven.[37] But if American academic musical culture accepted this metaphorical extension of "literacy," it quickly also associated it with the more explicit traditional definition of literacy, the ability to "read" music. The quotation marks are intended to remind readers that reading music means everything from looking at a score and roughly understanding its characteristics to being able to perform a piece while looking at the score for the first time, much as one may read out loud a verbal passage as one is first exposed to it.

To Music Building society, the concept of musical notation is enormously important. Having perhaps forgotten that they learned their first songs by hearing them, many of the denizens cannot conceive of a musical culture that does not use notation, and until recently many of my colleagues were inclined to marvel at my account of Indian musicians' improvising interestingly for an hour, or of Blackfoot Indians' maintaining a repertory of hundreds of songs, keeping them separate and knowing which go where in rituals, without any visual mnemonics. Among the many legendary stories about Mozart are two—his excellence as an improviser and his ability to write down or perform at the keyboard music he had heard but not seen—that attest to his near-supernatural character because they show how little he had to depend on notation.

Music to Music Building society is *notated* music. The homology of the words—"music" as a central concept and "music" as a body of notations—is illustrative, as is the unwillingness of teachers and administrators to mix music-reading majors in a class with other students who presumably do not read music. At the same time, classical musicians distinguish readily between the "notes" and "the music," saying to their students, for example, "You're just playing the notes, but not the music."[38] But American academic musical culture readily fits into the academic practice of using the metaphorical extension of literacy as indicating knowledge of one's culture; it is hard for professors of music to accept that one can understand music without using notation.

How a society transmits its culture, how a musical system transmits itself, is of enormous importance for understanding the society's character.[39] The concept of transmission is a complicated matter. Viewing European music through the prism of technology, we find at least four kinds of transmission: oral or aural (you learn music from hearing it in live performance, and quite likely any two performances may differ slightly—or greatly); written (you learn music from a unique notated version that may differ from every other copy of that notation, and each person learning that piece may receive it from a different and slightly variant copy); printed (everyone learning a piece may learn it from an identical notation); and recorded (you learn a piece from hearing it, but you can hear it the same way every time).[40] In some ways, oral and written traditions are alike, as are printed and recorded.

But what then is transmitted? The answer depends on the ways in which music is perceived. We should ascertain whether a performer is required to play a piece *exactly* as he or she learns it, whether changes are permitted, whether there are interpretive choices, or even whether there is the requirement that a piece be altered every time it is rendered. The cultures of the world vary greatly in their answers to these questions, and an ethnomusicologically oriented history of European music would take them into account more than has usually been done.

The centrality of notation to Western music has many causes. Notation is necessary for the coordination of forces in complex ensembles, essential to the development of complex musical relationships. It is also a major factor in differentiating, or separating, music and musicians from their audiences. On the one hand, it is a meta-language for the musicians, who are strangers in a way to the rest of society because they read music (while nonmusicians claim to be musically ignorant, illiterate because of lacking this kind of reading skill); it is a meta-language because various musicians can communicate with each other and play in the same orchestra, even when they do not share a language. It is also a separating device in the sense that it enables individual musicians in orchestras or bands to play their parts without knowing what sound will emerge or how the entire work sounds. Notation has made it possible to produce music with important structures and relationships that the audience cannot hear or perceive but are ascertained only through visual analysis of the work.

In a culture that often wants to eat its cake and have it too, the orchestra, which produces the most beloved and prestigious of sounds, is—in its total dependence on score with its constraints and complexities—the musical phenomenon most distant and mysterious. But Mozart, beloved and mysterious among composers, is seen as the "supreme genius of music" in some measure because he could free himself from these constraints and make music that moved directly from his mind to the keyboard, showing that if need be, he could chuck it all and produce his music without notation.

Program Patterns

If the orchestra is a kind of factory or plantation for producing great music or an army for exhibiting perfection on the parade ground, it is principally in the service of the great masters. The content and structure of programs shed light on the significance of hierarchy and the hegemony of great masters. The order of pieces in a concert program is determined in part by the nature of the repertory. String quartet concerts, which perforce consist of several pieces of about the same length, are inevitably different from orchestra concerts, which are expected to have several pieces of quite different lengths. Program structure is also substantially a matter of the personal preference of conductors and impresarios. Even so, patterns can be identified. At a concert of the London Philharmonic Society in 1820, each half began with a symphony and ended with an overture; the middle sections were comprised of areas, a concerto, a violin obligato, and a string quartet. However great the variety of programs in North America might be during the period from 1950 to 1990, this structure seems totally out of question. Almost as strange would be the form of an 1884 concert that took place in Kassel and began with four works by Louis Spohr, included two full-length symphonies, three opera overtures, a concerto, and Brahms's "Variations on a Theme by Haydn." Overtures began and closed the event, flanking the symphonies, with the rest of the music in the middle, all in a concert rather longer than what American audiences of the 1990s would ordinarily tolerate.[41]

Examination of a large sample of concert programs from the 1930s to the 1980s yields a principal pattern and several secondary ones. In the early part of the period, patterns in American orchestra concerts and solo recitals were relatively consistent; since then, greater variety has been established, driven perhaps by competing values. But in midcentury, the concert program of a symphony orchestra typically had (1) an overture or introductory piece, possibly by a Baroque composer, usually by a small version of the orchestra; (2) the pièce de résistance, a symphony by a great master; (3) flexibility after the intermission by means of a piece of twentieth-century music or possibly a concerto; and (4) a lighter number or group. Departures from such patterns seem to have been most pronounced in the greatest of orchestras and also in the least distinguished of academic ensembles, and consistency was greatest at the center.[42] The spot after the overture clearly seems the most exposed because late-comers would miss the overture; the intermission, an obligatory and essentially social event without which a classical concert can hardly be tolerated, would signal the beginning of a denouement. Variations of the pattern are common and often seem determined by certain consistent criteria, such as the value of chronology, the degree to which a conductor wishes to emphasize an interest in new music, the prestige of a violin or piano soloist, and the difficulty—for either orchestra or audience—of a major work (such as a symphony by Mahler or Bruckner), which might cause it to occupy the entire second half. But the fact that there was one pattern of greatest currency is significant, as is the very existence of program patterns governed by values such as hierarchy, duality, the importance of a rather rigid taxonomy, and the tension between supernatural genius and human accomplishment.

In other cultures, concert traditions—to say nothing of religious and social rituals requiring music—have their own patterns that similarly suggest guiding musical and social principles. In a concert of the classical music of South India, the multisectioned improvised number called *ragam-tanam-pallavi* begins just after the midpoint, although there is usually no intermission. In Persian classical music, the conceptually central and most prestigious section, the improvised *Âvâz*, appears in the very center of the full-blown performance.

As outlined in his well-known book on the American symphony orchestra, which analyzes the concert programs of twenty orchestras over several decades, John Mueller's "big four" (Beethoven, Brahms, Tchaikovsky, and Mozart), whose work occupies some 40 percent of symphonic playing time, were almost invariably the composers of the pièces de résistance.[43] There are no precise figures for recent decades, and although the mentioned degree of standardization has no doubt been softened in North America, the hierarchical structure of programs has been maintained, and the great masters occupy the top (the spot before the intermission) and also provide the "great" (longest) pieces.

The Great Masters and Cultural Values

The structure and function of art music in the Music Building can be variously interpreted. It reflects not only a political and economic elite by being the music of this segment of society but also by itself lording it over other musics on account of its structural complexity and sophistication. It is the "natural" musical component of a culture in which technology and technical complexity otherwise dominate. It goes with a culture (the absence of respect for improvisation notwithstanding) in which individual achievement and doing the difficult are highly prized and rewarded. The taxonomy of musics within which it is placed reflects the taxonomy of society. It is the "ethnic" music of a sector of the population, but in other respects it is the music that has no ethnic home, old music that is loved by a population that otherwise knows little of its own past.

The interpretation of the world of the Music Building as analogous to a religious system seems suggestive because of the domination in that world by a pantheon similar to those of certain religious systems. Deities give musical and behavioral principles to guide us. Rituals dominate society and require the best known, although not the best, music. What this society wishes most is large amounts of goods and services to consume and complex machinery for life and play, and thus the great composers are most respected when they produce musical works of almost incredible sophistication, complexity, and length.

Ethnomusicologists see music as a constituent part of culture, with reflections, homologies, and symbols. In many cultures, music functions to associate humans with the supernatural, and virtually all religious systems include music as a major component. The Music Building community sees music as a supernatural force to be worshipped and also as a system whose deities reign and require obedience. One Heartland music school in which I taught began each academic year with a short ceremony that ended with the hymnlike singing of Schubert's song "An die Musik" (To Music). Although this worshipful attitude toward the center of classical music is obligatory within the Music Building, those outside it (such as the viewers of commercials for wine, stylish furniture, or expensive coffee) also incline to it, sensing that it embodies, like religion and perhaps in exaggerated form, certain guiding principles of society: hierarchy, specialization, the drive to complexity, the tension between inspiration and labor, conformity, and more. But like certain supernatural forces, it is also feared and therefore marginalized, considered intelligible only to the specialist.

In the pantheon, in the central repertory, and as embodiment of the myths that dominate the Music Building, the figure of Mozart is the central paradigm, representing to many musicians a watershed of the best and also the most "normal" from which they look backward and forward. Understanding not Mozart the historical figure but Mozart the hero of twentieth-century Western musical mythology is fundamental to understanding the ways of the mind in Music Building society.

A principal reason for Mozart's preeminence is his identification with the concept of genius, a concept representing the extreme form of the notion of "talent" that is, as Kingsbury repeatedly points out, so essential to the existence of the Western art music system and that associates it, despite its prevailing secular nature, to the divine. The Mozart of twentieth-century biography, the Mozart of myth, is the man loved by God, *Amadeus*—as he is named by the playwright Peter Shaeffer, a sobriquet that came to be popularly applied in the late 1980s—virtually a supernatural figure.[44] Mozart's music must be played as he himself would have wished it, and departure from the supposed eighteenth-century norms is regarded by some music lovers as treasonous—greatly in contrast to the many styles, interpretations, and costumes of the twentieth-century world of Shakespearean performance. But for a composer today to write seriously in the style of Mozart is unacceptable to the world of the Music Building, not because people no longer like that kind of music but because ordinary humans should emulate yet not imitate the deities. Despite the rational analytical and frequently positivistic approach of scholars, music, more than the other arts, is seen in Heartland Music Building society as inexplicable, and the master musician is a strange person, a foreigner, or a supernatural figure in special relationship with God or in league with the devil.

Contrary to the Mozart of the eighteenth century, who wrote music for patrons and occasions, most of those who inhabit the Music Building tend to see their music as "art for art's sake" and not as part of everyday life. But to ethnomusicologists who analyze their own musical culture from an outsider's perspective, the perspective conventional in this field, Western art music is by no means separable from its cultural context. As an interrelated system of musical works and practices, social behavior, and ideas about music, it is structured with the use of principles built on the same dimensions that structure Western society at large. Identifying certain of these principles makes clear the culturally situated nature of the great Western art music tradition.

In this system of Western culture that produces wonderful music, what are the principles and values that are expressed and that underlie it? Here are intriguing concepts such as genius, discipline, efficiency, the hierarchical pyramid of musics and composers, the musician as stranger and outsider, the wonders of complexity, the stimulus of innovation, and music as a great thing with metaphorical extensions. But we are also forced to suggest dictatorship, conformity, a rigid class structure, overspecialization, and a love of mere bigness are all explicitly or by implication extolled. Why do the denizens of the Music Building love so well a kind of music that grows from principles they would probably dismiss as characteristic of an unkind society? One may counter that the analysis is faulty, that instead of conformity there is cooperation, instead of authoritarians there are leaders. Or argue that the kind of social structure described, for all its undesirable aspects, is essential for the proper performance of music by the great masters, that in order for music of such an incredibly elite character as that of Mozart's or Beethoven's to be created and performed one must simply sacrifice independence and personal opinion, must undertake an incredible amount of discipline and accept dictates of an elite wherever they lead. And yet the ethnomusicologist from Mars has discovered questions but is far from providing definitive answers.

∾ 2 ∾

Society of Musicians

Music Communities

The great Carnatic singer and his accompanists—on violin and percussion instruments—were moving through their concert with almost
incredible smoothness. Each musician had a role, and the interaction
was perfect. But underneath it, the Madras insider may tell you, it's
all competition and even conflict. Musically, the singer is supreme,
singing composed songs or improvising in his interpretation, and he
is specifically accompanied by the two-headed drum, mridangam,
with which he sometimes competes. In other ways, he is also accompanied by another competitor, the violinist, whose excellence is determined by his ability to follow and repeat the singer's improvised
phrases most precisely. But when soloing, the violin is accompanied
by the clay-pot percussion instrument, the *ghatam,* and the mridangam solos are accompanied by the *ghatam* as well. It and the violin
vie for the role of first accompanist. The tamboura, the large lute
playing the drone, is lowest in status but musically most essential.

No two performers enjoy musically equal status. Nor are these
musicians equal in their nonmusical lives, because differences in caste,
professional status, and gender all play major roles. Singers are almost
always high-caste Brahmins, violinists and mridangam players less
frequently so, and other musicians are even more likely to be from
lower castes. Singers are sometimes women, less frequently violinists, virtually never percussionists, but, in any event, male accompanists have been known to feel there is something not quite right about

accompanying a woman. Sometimes the low-caste drummer is universally recognized, and the audience gives him anomalously high status over the high-caste singer. Or perhaps the lowly *ghatam* player is the son and student of a towering musical figure, member of a great lineage of musicians, disturbing the system in yet another way. At the end of the concert, the chief guest bestows garlands on the musicians. In what order? Usually it's no problem, but sometimes he must juggle considerations of standard musical structure, social standing, musical reputation, and gender and finds there is no way of being fair; there are so many conflicting criteria, so many levels of interaction.[1]

The inhabitants of a Heartland university school of music also relate to each other and interact in many ways.[2] My purpose is to contemplate the social relations among some of the many groups that comprise this population—students and teachers and administrators, beginners and advanced, players and singers, strings and winds, men and women, majorities and minorities, conductors and the conducted—both as members of American society and academic society at large and in their roles as members of the music profession. It seems to me that a small and specific set of principles of social organization govern the relationships among people in the Music Building in their everyday contacts, and that these same principles govern their relationships in their roles as musicians, particularly in ensembles. Furthermore, these principles also help to illuminate the association among structural components of Western art music such as the order of events in concerts, the relationship of parts in ensembles, and of ensembles to each other. As suggested further in chapter 4, Music Building society to some degree perceives its musical repertory, and the relationships among its components such as works and genres, in ways derived from its conception of human society. The inhabitants of the Music Building see themselves and their work in terms of certain values and, like the musicians of Madras, of the tensions among opposing principles.

The perspective, I suggest, has been long established in ethnomusicology. Daniel Neuman has also approached the understanding of Indian classical musics by suggesting that important characteristics of Indian society—relationships and competition among caste groups and other subdivisions of society, importance of nuclear and extended family, significance of obligation and exchange, and relationship between age and gender groups—tell one a great deal about musical life and style.[3] The particular characteristics of a "jazz community" as one whose social and musical interrelationships intersect were the subject of spirited discussion early on in ethnomusicology. Alan Lomax tried to show that the quality of relationships among people in a society is reflected in the interrelationships of components in their ensembles. Anthony Seeger examined the ways in which social structure directly influences musical structure in a small tribal society, while Christopher Waterman analyzed ways in which Nigerian juju music reflects important aspects of Yoruba social organization and its dynamics. Working in Iran, I tried to show that typical and ideal relationships among different sorts of individuals have parallels in the relationship among components of the classical music system.[4] Thus my examination of Heartland U. Music Building society is actually part of a long-standing ethnomusicological tradition.

The Principal Classes

Students, Teachers, and Administrators

The individuals who spend their working days in the Music Building probably consider themselves members of several population groups and nodes in several types of human relationships. But in the first instance they typically identify themselves as members of one of three classes: students, teachers, and administrators. For a good many people, these categories are clear and easy to establish, but there are also significant ways in which the lines of demarcation are vague. Some persons partake of two or even three of the functions, both officially and in their personal perception. Teachers see themselves as eternal students and scholars, and, more than in other university departments, the younger ones have perhaps actually been pupils of the older ones. The students move gradually from exclusiveness of study to partial teaching. Some become student teachers in public schools, others assist teachers in the music school even as undergraduates, and many become graduate teaching assistants. Age may play a role in self-perception and self-classification. In music more than in other academic fields, academics become full-time university teachers while still completing their degrees. Even so, the tripartite grouping is the most important one, the one that most determines forms of behavior and affects other components of the Music Building's social taxonomy.

The three categories and their relationships reflect, in substance and form, significant structures of social organization found widely in American society: the tripartite system of socioeconomic classes used in informal terminology; the separation of management, labor, and customers in businesses and industry; and the hierarchies of military and athletic organizations. Important as well, although less precisely, they parallel the organization of the paradigmatic Western music ensembles, orchestra, chorus, and band. The three categories—administrators, teachers, and students—are naturally also the main ones in American academia. But the separation between administrator and teacher is greater in the field of music, and the association of teacher and student closer than that found in higher education at large. Music school social organization is more inclined than the rest of academia to reflect the norms of American (indeed, older European) social structures, governments, corporations, and armies.

I will begin by commenting on the relationship of the classes of the Music Building to socioeconomic classes as conventionally and informally described.[5] Officially and formally, administrators (whom I'll call alternatively "dean," "director," or "head," reflecting the multiple terminology at universities) are simply teachers who have moved into roles of leadership, sometimes just temporarily. Some actually do continue to teach while holding administrative jobs, or else they perform or publish. In any event, in the inevitable moments of adversity they may console themselves with the thought that they may return to "full-time teaching" or even, via receiving grants or working on additional degrees, to a life in which they can devote themselves to study, research, or composing.

In fact, few music administrators, once established in their positions, return to teaching, and when they are obliged or choose to do so, it is regarded as a demotion. Indeed, Music Building people have a rather unified conception of the model professional career. Most generally, they envision a sequence derived from the ideals of American culture: student to teacher to administrator. A sequence regarded by society at large as quite normal, it parallels the rise of an apprentice to valued worker to member of the management team and finally perhaps owner of a business. At the same time, this conception of the ideal career seems to be realized less frequently in other academic fields. The typical history or sociology professor expects to go from study to teaching and remain there, rising in the profession by becoming a famous scholar and occupying endowed chairs, by receiving teaching positions in which one does relatively little teaching, or by perhaps getting a "research professorship." In a typical college of liberal arts, professors become department heads or deans for a few years and then routinely "return to teaching and research" without considering this a demotion. To be sure, certain nonmusic professors do enter lower-level administration and remain there, but such positions are not usually stepping-stones to higher administration.

And so, professors of music—more, I believe, than others—strive to become department heads and deans, and the normal path to deanship may be via the ranks of assistant and associate dean (or director, or head). One distinguished music dean who was inclined (about 1950) to shock his colleagues with droll stories defined an associate dean as "a mouse trying to become a rat."

Music administrators see themselves as a distinct class. As suggested in the rat joke, the expression of raw power probably used to be more common among music administrators than among heads of humanistic and social science units. But even now, music deans and heads, referring to themselves as "music executives," associate with each other more in organizations than do other academic administrators, having in the United States created several organizations with virtually the same membership to permit frequent contacts—the NASM (National Association of Schools of Music), NAMESU (National Association of Music Executives of State Universities), and "Seven Springs" group (approximately ten major state, private, university-connected, and free-standing music schools and conservatories). Normally held at luxurious hotels, meetings of NASM resemble conventions of business executives much more than conventional academic conferences. They are properly meetings of "schools" more than individuals, with the administrators of the large, powerful schools exhibiting their hegemony in various ways, frequently being seen in the hotel foyers and meeting halls with retinues of two or three associate and assistant deans. The atmosphere suggests a kind of camaraderie more typical of chief executive officers or captains of industry than of academic administrators as a whole.

Among the three classes, it may be assumed that the highest, administrators, has an interest in the maintenance of the class structure and thus encourages the concept of classes within the rest of the population. They may encourage or even require in their subordinates greater adherence to the principles of the academic ladder. As a member of a university promotions committee I was repeatedly asked why the school of music never recommended junior faculty for "early promotion." For students, the system of prerequisites in the curriculum, of requirements to be met in order, and of the concept of admission to study with "deficiencies" may in part relate to the importance of having classes.

Also more than in the rest of academia, in music schools there is a widespread belief that careers require upward movement through a series of relatively distinct steps. Contrary to the popular image of musicians as people who care little for the conventions of society, live only for art, or are rebels who symbolize this role with sloppy dress and long hair, musicians in academia more frequently stress the importance of social categories as indicators of status and of stages in an order of events. The importance of chronological order is, after all, important to classical musicians in many ways: They identify music by when it was composed, they worry about order in programs, rehearsals, lessons, and they often seem to believe that sequence of events and proper timing should be major factors in planning and carrying out a career in the school of music.

As suggested, the importance of class structure in music schools (compared to other academic groups) may derive from a corporate structure in which each employee sees himself or herself on a ladder on which the rungs must be climbed in sequence. Conceivably, this may be related to the importance of the concept of chronological progression in the education of classical musicians, a system in which things must be learned in a particular order and in which the order of parts in events such as concerts, rehearsals, and practice sessions may be rigorously prescribed.

If the right order is often essential in the world of classical music, it may refer to an ordering in chronological terms, or in terms of value. Ideally, a musician moves from beginner to intermediate student, advanced student, beginning professional, full-fledged professional, master, and star. Few individuals follow this line precisely; some move from professional to nonperforming teacher, and few ever become stars. But many aspects of musical and social behavior underscore the existence of this continuum, along which one moves gradually. Special respect is given to individuals who move along the sequence rapidly, who become stars at an early age, and those who conflate or sweep aside the sequence, moving like Mozart from child prodigy to star performer, are sometimes treated as if their gifts had truly come from the supernatural.

The emphasis on an order in which the components of a musical system are learned by its practitioners is found in many cultures. A case in point is the need to learn certain songs when one is young and others at an advanced age in some Australian aboriginal societies, as is the importance of learning to play didjeridu when one is a young bachelor among the people of Yirkalla.[6] More like the Western classical system is the learning of the *radif* in Persian music, a canonic repertory of some three hundred pieces whose constituent parts and subdivisions should be learned in a specific order, the one called *Shur* coming first because it is the most important and the most characteristic of Persian music.

What comes first is not necessarily the most important everywhere. In the music of South India, there is much variety among master musicians in the order of teaching events, but each teacher may have his or her own unalterable method. Thus, S. Ramanathan habitually taught the raga *Mayamalavagaula* first because it has four semitones, so he said. And he insisted on practice sessions and lessons in which one began with scalar and rhythmic exercises, went on to etudelike *varnams,* and further to the complex devotional songs, the *kritis.* Indeed, the order of events is significant in the way the proper career of an Indian musician is perceived. One moves from various levels of studentship to a station more properly described as apprentice; begins, with the informal title of disciple, to accompany the teacher on trips and at concerts; and then goes on to become a soloist. In this progression, the acquisition of the musical system is monitored carefully. A musician's teacher may decide when it is proper for solo performance in public to begin, sometimes not until early middle age. The model for the order of events in a musician's career is extended to concern for its context because musicians in India are typically identified by their teachers and those teachers' own musical genealogy.

In the world of Western art music, order doesn't play such a definitive role. But a coherent career, a student's relationship with the principal teacher, a kind of ideal model of chronology, do play a substantial part. The importance of order in practicing (from technical to interpretive, from earlier music to recent) was formerly very important in pedagogy and is still maintained by some teachers, particularly those who teach beginning or intermediate students. ("First, play the scales!")[7] The continuum from easy to difficult and of compositional chronology are important in many of the ritual-like events that a musician undergoes, particularly while a student. The proper order of career events, especially if there is a context, is something to which musicians and their audiences pay great attention. Program notes typically inform about landmarks, discuss teachers, and make a point of a musical family background (usually with some suggested tone of satisfaction) and of early beginning of music study. It seems that ideal musicians come from families of musicians and begin study early.

The importance of chronological order helps to explain the importance of stages in the careers of academic musicians. The existence and order of the categories leading from beginner to star affect significant aspects of musical life in music schools, but the administrator-teacher-student sequence, and aspects of the industrial model to which it is related, are superimposed on the sequence of events in musicians' actual careers.

How then do music school denizens in different classes coexist and make music together? Looking at the practices that are followed in arranging performances, one notes that there are ensembles in which members of two of the categories perform together. But not just any two categories. Thus, teachers play with students and even accompany them. Administrators perform with teachers, and they may conduct students. But only if a student is certifiably a star will an administrator perform with him or her on equal terms, to say nothing of accompanying him or her. The great ability of a violin student whom I observed was established when his dean was persuaded to accompany him. A student might, on rare occasions, conduct an ensemble of students or of students and teachers but, in my experience, not one in which administrators are included.

Class structure plays a major role in determining who plays with whom and what roles each class may occupy. But it is important also that all three classes may be active in public performance, play the same repertory, and live together with sometimes rigid, sometimes imprecise boundaries.

The Industrial Model

In describing the relationship of the three main groups, comparison to industry or corporations turns out to be suggestive. Administrators (dean or director and also associate and assistant deans, often junior in their relationship to teachers and with little professional accomplishment) have the task of raising funds (from benefactors or the legislature), seeking a market of customers (recruiting students and advertising), and hiring labor. Professors are the labor force. They may be highly skilled, specialized, and influential, but in the end assigning them activities and determining their remuneration are tasks that fall to administrators. It is true that in their details these activities are left to them to a high degree. Professors' teaching methods are not supervised, they select repertory for their own performances and for those of their students, and the daily schedule is largely left to their discretion. But they are much less frequently expected to face the outside world on behalf of the institution than are the administrators, and they do not get as much involved in the acquisition of customers. It is, for example, the administrators who in the end decide how many students, and which ones, may be admitted and what kinds of teachers will be hired.

In the industrial model, the students are customers as well as products. As customers, they buy instruction and degrees, and they determine which instruction and which degrees to buy in terms of the relative cost and quality. Cost includes not only tuition but also—and perhaps even more—the amount of effort and time that must be spent. Prerequisites—course and recital requirements, residence obligations, and difficulty of examinations—all figure in the calculation of the "price" that must be paid for the degree. They are discussed with faculty and administrators before one embarks on a study program, much as the qualities of a house or car are discussed by seller and buyer. Contact with "satisfied customers" such as older students and alumni plays a role in recruiting. Once in school, many students feel that they are not after all being treated like valued customers by labor or management; in fact, however, attention is given to their sensitivities. It is a matter of determining the nature of the transaction. Tuition pays for instruction, but "paying" professors by practicing and doing homework is mainly what will buy the degree.

The Heartland U. music school also has other classes of customers: audiences at performances; the body academic, which needs music to sanctify its rituals of graduation, baccalaureate, and athletics; and the university administration, which uses the school of music as one of its attractions to more valuable faculty such as professors of engineering and sciences, the people whose ability to attract grants is central to the economic well-being of the institution.

What then of the products of the music school if it is seen as an industrial organization? In part, it produces performances: recitals, concerts and operas, marching band shows, and also new compositions, theses, and works of scholarship. It is uniquely among musical institutions in society that the product of schools of music is conceived to be well-trained graduates. Music administrators talk about "producing good students," and the concept and the term *selling* play a role in the use of magazine and journal advertising, in extolling the famous teachers who may (or may not) have been the mentors of the "products," in tireless attempts to get the name of the institution into print in any way possible, in encouraging the attendance of students and teachers at professional and scholarly conferences in order to meet prospective "customers," and much else parallel to traditional business techniques. Like a sales organization, the music school permits its administrators, the white-collar force, to do most of the selling, or at least to supervise it. The school's job is to prove that the degrees are worthwhile by helping students find jobs, an activity on which no small effort is expended.

I have noted ways in which the taxonomy of musics is reflected in the costumes of performers, but when not playing music in public the three classes of music school society, like most social divisions in Western society, tend to distinguish themselves—although not uniformly—by dress or costume. Administrators usually dress formally, being careful to maintain the image of white-collar workers, and in conformity with the tendency of sales personnel to dress in suit and tie. Male teachers dress in a variety of ways, sometimes formally in suits, sometimes as informally as students, but most commonly during the 1980s it was colored shirts, sports jackets, sweaters, and the absence of necktie that comprised the characteristic academic-labor attire. There is less difference in dress between female administrators and teachers, as both groups tend to dress rather formally.

To classes and lessons, and for practice and rehearsal, students usually wear distinctive but not uniform outfits emphasizing informality. Blue jeans and embossed or imprinted T-shirts or sweatshirts, cut-off shorts in spring, sneakers, and sometimes sandals or thongs were the norms around 1990. This is students' "customer" attire; as customers, they need not impress anybody, daring teachers to impress them. In their role of "products," when they perform music in public, engage in student teaching, and interview for jobs, they wear "product" costumes, conforming to the norms of dress in the world of music outside the Music Building and showing that they are indeed products ready to be hired, to be purchased by the real world.

Three Kinds of Coin

Each of the three classes has its function in the school's musical and educational system, and the entire enterprise is cooperative, but students, teachers, and administrators also maneuver for power, occasionally allying themselves, two against one, in Orwellian oppositions not unique to 1984. Thus, students and teachers combine to pressure administrators for special favors—a university van to go to an out-of-town concert, new instruments, higher pay for teachers and assistants, more scholarship money for students. Teachers and administrators in turn may pressure students for higher fees, but much more typically they combine under another banner, to increase the students' role in the common enterprise whose quintessence is concerts. Thus, they may require students to perform (perhaps imposing the so-called ensemble requirements, which oblige students to enroll in ensembles throughout their course of study) and to attend as members of the audience (imposing a similar "recital requirement").

Administrators and students, in turn, sometimes join as well. They may try to motivate teachers to give more attention to their teaching and to make themselves more available. Sometimes they pressure teachers to permit exceptions from the academic rule book, such as loosening requirements. A voice major whose fine voice is essential for opera productions, the apple of the dean's eye but untalented as a theory student, may have a theory grade raised as a result of administrative suggestion. These interactions provide a certain equilibrium among the three groups, a system of checks and balances.

The most important factor separating the three groups, however, is a system of rewards that uses conventional money and also academic and musical coin. Students, as the principal customers, pay to be part of the enterprise; or, payment is made by their representatives, parents or state legislatures. But they are paid, as well, in ways that are obvious but usefully explained as part of the reciprocal relationships among the three classes.

When paid in standard coin, as in the case of teaching assistants, library helpers, or stage hands, the remuneration is much less than that of teachers (or librarians or professional stage hands), even when the activities are identical. But students may also be paid in standard coin for excellence of performance—normally musical performance in the literal sense, that is, playing and singing—through scholarships and occasionally fees for concerts.

Administrators are the most successful recipients of standard coin, being paid better than teachers and receiving bonuses; for example, more of their travel and entertainment costs are paid. Some of them feel—and this perception may be shared by the other classes—that they "are" the institution to a greater extent than the teachers or the student body. They are the ones who control the financial world of the schools and determine budgets, salaries, and expenditures. They are also normally employed to work through the calendar year, whereas teachers may or may not receive summer employment. Music administrators, talking to each other, frequently refer to "my oboe teacher" and "my ethnomusicologist," in rhetoric reminiscent of owners of businesses or athletic teams.

When it comes to academic coin, music schools are like other units at Heartland U. Departments such as history or English consist of faculty members who teach classes, advise dissertation and other independent student research, and engage in research, reading papers, and writing. Their position in the hierarchy is determined by the quantity and significance of their research, the excellence or popularity of their teaching, their service or leadership in university affairs as exhibited in committee work, and their acceptance of administrative duties. Academic rewards are titles (such as "university professor" or "university scholar"), endowed chairs, honorary degrees, travel funds, released time, and promotion. The rewards may be accompanied by money but clearly have their own value. Bestowing them is largely in the hands of administrators (to be sure, with requirements of advice, but not always consent, of faculty committees). Students have a small role in determining how teachers will be rewarded, but to them academic coin is very important; it is grades and titles such as "summa cum laude."

In music schools, the system of rewards also includes something we could call "musical coin," in which teachers and administrators, and, indeed, students, are paid. Translatable into academic and standard coin, it nevertheless has an existence of its own because in the conception of music school inhabitants, there is some ambivalence about the degree to which artists should be guided by the standards of ordinary American society. On one side of their psyche, musicians want to be paid well, to make money, but they may also feel that they are somehow above the material world and that the opportunity of making music, that gift from the supernatural, is its own reward. The concept is expressed in such statements as the famous musician's commencement address devoted largely to telling the graduates that they are the luckiest of people; the willingness of musicians to perform without being paid in money; and the stated purpose of the musical profession as one whose service is not mainly to humans, but to the abstract (and maybe sacred) concept of music.

What this means, in practical terms, is being permitted to perform, or being in demand as a performer. In general, musicians wish to perform, and so getting opportunities to play or sing (or to have their compositions performed, or perhaps their articles published) is the normal remuneration. Artists in other fields—painters, actors, dancers, and writers—live in similar systems. But in music there is also a higher reward (or payment) that revolves about the values in the classical music system and the dual role of the music school as a teaching institution and an entertainment arm of the university. The reward is to be appointed to positions of leadership in musical organization and the hierarchical system they represent, because the highest reward in musical coin is to be permitted to conduct the music-making of others.

Classes of Musicianship

Those Who Can, Do: Performers and Academics

Members of music school society identify and classify themselves and the components of their world in a number of ways. In the previous section, I represented the principal taxonomy as a kind of ladder. For other aspects of the system the opposition of center and periphery are more appropriate. Thus, there are central and peripheral kinds of music in the music school's repertory (Mozart versus Kurt Weill), central and peripheral instruments (piano versus guitar), types of activity (playing music versus reading about music), and perhaps even degrees (B.M. versus A.B., the degree of committed performers as opposed to the degree of dilettantes or of students preparing for a career in scholarship). Among activities, performance is seen as central by music school society, and there are those who perform and those who don't. The grouping and status are encapsulated by a frequently heard maxim: "Those who can, do; others teach [or write books]."

Among the violinists or pianists of the art music world, there is a bit of competitive one-upmanship between professors who nevertheless give concerts and concert artists who give some private lessons. To musicians outside the academy, all members of a music faculty may in a sense be people who cannot really do, otherwise they wouldn't teach. One looks down on them but also fears them, because they are, in a way, the enemy. They have the job security of tenure, and they make it a requirement for others who wish to enter into the institutional teaching profession—at college or school level—to come to them for certification. Some public- or private-sector musicians regard the teaching profession as a bureaucracy for maintaining artificial standards, but overriding this animosity they almost inevitably have great loyalty to their former teachers.

Within the Music Building, the center, the people who do, is largely comprised of the performing faculty and student majors, and the periphery consists of those who—broadly speaking—teach without performing, ordinarily faculty and students of music education, musicology, and music theory. Composers are in a somewhat anomalous position. They obviously do, but they work, like teachers and scholars, on paper; unlike performers, they are not expected to undertake the risks that exposure to an audience constantly demands. Their accomplishments are not physical, like those of performers, and as composers they do not practice. Performers may imitate each other, but composers may only emulate.

Many performers of classical music do not take contemporary composers seriously. Their attitude has to do with the experimental character and requirement of innovativeness, which also requires flexibility and adaptability on the part of listeners. At bottom, there is a performer's ideal of music as the work of the great masters. Performers see themselves (and are seen by the general and academic public) as central because they perform the works of the great masters who rule the system.

Some music schools in the Heartland have rationalized their structure by reducing their subdivisions to two, a division of performance and one of "academic studies" or "academic studies and composition," which puts composers in the same category as music historians, theorists, and educators. Because composition is usually taught in private lesson format, the distinction between class and private instruction as the main criterion is not explanatory. We still must return to the conception of doing as performance and as a principal criterion.

In fact, most composers do practice, perform, and do difficult things on instruments, and they are known in the music school for this. In the Heartland U. Music Building in 1990, 80 percent of the composers had some solistic participation in at least one public performance, although in many cases it was to perform their own compositions. This cannot be said of the musicologists and music education faculty, who, as a group, had only a 35 percent performance ratio.

There is a good deal of conflict and competition between the performers—faculty and students—and the rest. It is obvious that performers regard themselves as the central portion of the school and that the school's administration shares this view. Nonperformers are expected to attend concerts and recitals by performing students and faculty, but performers are typically not urged to attend concerts of new music or lectures and papers by scholars, or to read their publications. The university public as a whole sees performers as the quintessence of the school. The performers are also the majority.

Nevertheless, there are ways in which nonperformers as a group may hold positions of considerable power. Thus, students of performance are required to take courses in theory, music history, and, in some curricula, music education methods courses; in effect, all students in the school must take some nonperforming courses. The opposite is also true, although to a smaller extent: Students entering graduate study in performance must show background and ability in the academic subjects, but specialists in music history and education need not pass muster as performers. (Whether there are substantive reasons that have nothing to do with power relations may be debated, but the difference in treatment often rankles among performing faculty and students who, seeing themselves as central, nevertheless feel disenfranchised by this perceived inequality.) By the same token, doctoral students in performance must carry out academic research; their doctoral committees must include faculty from among the scholars. But doctoral students in scholarly areas need not show their ability to perform, and performance faculty are not on their committees. It is true that students outside the performing major areas have performance requirements such as participation in ensembles, but to impose these, the performance faculty have had to plead the importance of the school's function as a provider of entertainment for the community.

Performers thus see musicologists as a kind of police, imposing music history requirements on their students, making them take entrance examinations, and otherwise forcing them to jump through hoops of (they think) an essentially irrelevant sort in defense of an obsolete and ephemeral canon. They may see little need for their students to know about medieval and Renaissance music, or about the music of India and China.

The two groups thus struggle for hegemony, which may be expressed in the identity and background of the dean or head. Is he or she a performer and, if so, with a Ph.D.? Or an academic but with a performer's credentials? Occasionally, in making an appointment, the higher administration tries to find individuals who can be presented as "double threats" and show this to the public. Thus, in one famous (non-Heartland) music school, the new administrator had an inauguration ceremony at which he read a scholarly paper, performed as a pianist, and conducted an orchestra. At other schools, the academic credentials of the performing head are emphasized by the insistence that he or she be called "doctor."

Within the large groups of performers and academics there are subdivisions that compete for control and prestige, usually in a context of substantial collegiality. Within the academic branch, the struggle is frequently between music historians and music educators, again somewhat under the rubric of the criterion of "those who can, do." Many music educationists regard themselves as practical professionals striving to do a job required by society. They have learned what is needed and have little time for the esoteric pursuits of historians, and they expect less course work in music history for their students than do other curricula. When educationists request help from musicologists for solution of their problems, they find themselves constantly frustrated by the historians' unwillingness to look at things their way. They are also convinced that many music historians do not teach well and have little concern for quality of teaching, accusing them of steering their own graduate students away from those music education courses in which they might learn something about teaching. At the level of research, music educators see themselves as scientists who, with the use of techniques from social sciences and psychology, learn what is needed to solve practical problems. They, too, regard musicologists as a kind of police who impose course requirements, which they have sometimes combated by establishing a degree of academic autonomy.

Some musicologists, in turn, see music educators as philistines who do not wish to teach the best music and the highest values to their students, who ignore the many kinds of things that musicologists could teach them, and who are not really interested in the music itself. At some institutions, musicologists point out that the attendance of music educators—faculty and students—at local concerts is lower than that of any other area in music. The generally low esteem of the public school teaching profession in the United States is brought into play. The smaller quantity of humanistic courses and language requirements in music education curricula is criticized as incompatible with the aims of the university as a whole.

Each group—music educationists and musicologists—occasionally sides with performers and seeks their support. In recent times at Heartland U., music educators sided with performers in imposing the requirement that students participate in ensembles. But musicologists have consistently joined performers in approving foreign language requirements that do not apply in music education. Within the "academic" group there is continuing competition without a consistent hierarchical result. Yet within the university as a whole, as measured by such criteria as membership on university committees, awards for research, or honorary degrees, there seems to have been a trend, beginning in the 1950s, to move leadership away from music education to the fields of musicology and composition. The change may correlate with changes in the role of teaching in higher education and with the changing equilibrium between teaching and research as concepts in American society.

"What Do You Play?": Singers and Players

If the struggle between musicology and music education is paradigmatic of academia and predictable within the academic realm of the Music Building, other less obvious struggles within the realm of performance study and teaching are probably more significant in providing insight into the character of Western art music culture within the realm of the performers. First, there are singers and instrumentalists.

The distinction between vocal and instrumental music is important throughout Western musical culture; it also plays a major role in the Middle East and India. In South Indian classical music, the musical system is quintessentially vocal; instruments imitate the voice, and singers are the musicians of greatest prestige. In the Islamic Middle East, with its ambivalent conception of music, vocal music is less threatening than instrumental and in some manifestations is not regarded as "music." But in contemporary North America or Western Europe, one hears the question, "You're a musician? What do you play?" defining music as quintessentially instrumental.

The struggles for dominance within the performing portion of the music school intersect significantly with perceived and actual contrasts in gender roles in culture and music.[8] It is thus appropriate to make a brief foray into this widely studied field. Europe, South India, and Iran hold fundamentally different attitudes toward music, toward the relative centrality of singing or instrumental music, and toward the relative participation of men and women in music. Yet in all three, vocal music is more associated with women than is instrumental music. Women sing more than they play, and most playing is done by men. In Carnatic music, l'Armand and l'Armand have documented women's greater participation in singing, their occasional playing of melody-producing instruments, and their relative absence in the world of percussion.[9] In Iranian classical and popular music (as experienced around 1970), women sing but hardly ever play, and, again, the occasional appearance of the instrumentalist is in the melodic rather than percussive function. Women are more likely to play the instruments that "sing."

The correlation is not universal, as women do play drums in some societies and, of course, do so now in Western culture. But women's association with vocality is widely regarded as a specialty, whereas the relative monopoly of males over instruments may be symbolic of male political domination and may be related to traditional male control over large, complex tools, particularly over weapons. Thus, the devout government of Iran during the 1970s was concerned specifically with forbidding women to sing in public. And in the Carnatic music culture of Madras, where some women musicians are highly honored, well-known percussionists may nevertheless feel insecure when invited to accompany female singers and may insist on being first in the small ceremony of garlanding that takes place after a concert and in which the hierarchy of musicianship is asserted.

In contemporary Western culture, the distinction is less pronounced and receding but nevertheless there. Men hold the majority of positions in orchestras, but women account for more than half the professional singers (in choruses and opera companies) in art music. The majority of conductors are men. Until recently, the women in the art music field who did not sing were typically pianists and string players; much less recently they were wind players; even now it is not common for them to be percussionists. The differences have been in some measure mitigated, but they are still present. In art music, however, the venue of greatest hospitality is the voice.[10] This is also true in popular music and jazz. Rock groups have more female vocalists than instrumentalists; the norm is a group of male guitar players, a male percussionist, and a female vocalist who plays "easier" instruments when needed, tambourine or keyboard chording. A typical jazz ensemble is male; a big band of men may have a woman singer.

Several factors mitigate the same relationships in the Music Building. Over some forty years there has been a gradual increase of women in instrumental music at large, beginning with piano and strings, moving to flute and then other woodwinds, eventually to brass, and then to percussion. The changes were probably first stimulated by the interest of many female students in becoming public school teachers—long a characteristically female profession—some of whom had to specialize in instruments, including winds. In the 1950s, teachers of vocal and "general" music were still likely to be women, whereas men usually taught instrumental music, especially winds; even more, men were conductors of orchestras and bands. Since 1970, concern with civil rights, feminism, and sexual politics has led to more rapid movement of women students into areas earlier almost exclusively the provinces of men. Throughout, however, one possible outlet for women's interest in instrumental music has remained the profession of teaching children.

As expected, the proportion of female students is greatest in the vocal department, followed closely by the string department.[11] So is the proportion of female teachers, as female voice teachers account for slightly more than half of the faculties of four Heartland schools. Given the uneven levels of esteem and prestige of the genders in American society, it might not be surprising that the instrument divisions generally have more esteem in the Music Building than the division of voice teachers.

Yet the relationship of vocal and instrumental music and musicians is complex. The two groups or areas, like performers and academics (and perhaps even like the Mozarts and Beethovens of the world), seem to engage in a struggle, again exhibiting the importance of duality and dichotomies in the culture of the Music Building. It is a struggle involving questions of athletic versus intellectual in music and also the significance of tools and technology. Ultimately, it is part of the debate about the relative value of natural talent and acquired skill, nature and culture, divine gift and human labor. Inevitably, the question of gender enters in.

In the belief system of instrumentalists (well, certain instrumentalists), singers may have beautiful natural voices but need not be highly intelligent; although the voice needs to be developed, singers need not learn manual skills. In my experience, it is true that singers often (and with significant exceptions) do worse than instrumentalists in academic subjects, whether from the tendency to select singers for the quality of voice, without consideration of other musical or academic talents, or from a nonintellectual self-image that singers acquire during their course of study. A good many graduate students majoring in singing, people who have excellent voices, find themselves deficient in the quality of their academic work—theory and music history—and must struggle for admission to the graduate programs of the school. They are supported by voice teachers and opera directors and opposed by the musicology or theory faculty, a kind of police force guarding academic standards, in a relationship parallel to that the music world accords to musicians employed in higher education. Singers' natural voices may see them through, but to instrumentalists they may have only talent, not skill.

In one peculiar sense at least, the vocal instruction system in the music school supports this interpretation. Typically, an instrumental student learns from his or her teacher how to play the instrument, how to play the music for the instrument, and how this music should sound—coeval treatment of technique and repertory. The same is often true of voice instruction, but some teachers emphasize the technique of singing and the development of the voice, leaving the study of vocal music and repertory to others—a staff of opera and lieder coaches, or teachers of accompanying (who, in fact, function as coach-accompanists). In addition, like other performing departments, the vocal department has a course on "vocal literature," which outlines and illustrates the repertory.

And so some instrumentalists have a scornful attitude toward vocalists: They must have their education stuffed into them by teachers because they cannot learn things by themselves. They have voice teachers for vocal technique; coach-accompanists to teach them the songs and other solo literature they will sing in recitals; opera coaches to teach them operatic roles; musicologists to teach them courses in vocal and choral literature; and choral conductors, who are more essential to performance than are orchestra conductors. Instrumentalists see themselves as more self-sufficient, having fewer teachers and depending on them less.

I have probably overstated it, but the instrumentalist's perspective reinforces many cultural stereotypes. Keep in mind that men are traditionally thought in this society to be better at handling tools (e.g., instruments) and better at the solving of intellectual problems, whereas women are "closer to nature" and more "emotional." The origin myths of Western music—dignified by the concept of "theory" but still mainly myth—may play a role here, as in the widespread belief that vocal music preceded the development of instrumental music and is thus more "natural," and that some thinkers believed it to have come from "emotional" speech and be thus closer to women.[12] Bear in mind also that the American musicians' union accepts instrumentalists but not vocalists (who are unionized with actors and dancers), and that along with women, male members of minority groups are more likely to be found in the vocal realm. The vernacular terminology deals with "musicians and singers." In a white, male-dominated, intellectually inclined, and technologically oriented society, it is easy to see why the vocal department may in some respects enjoy lower esteem.

All these distinctions have a merely marginal effect and are quickly submerged when more significant struggles dominate thought and action: the solidarity of music school versus the rest of the university, of the arts versus the sciences, and of art music versus pop and rock. And in any event, great artistic accomplishment raises a musician above stereotypes. The voice department may be low on the totem pole, but the diva on the faculty has great prestige throughout the university. Singers are not just a downtrodden class chafing under domination of strings and winds, and hierarchies and oppositions don't affect everyday life in music schools all the time. They must be ferreted out of a plethora of situations and incidents and behavior patterns.

The singers, in turn, fight back. They dominate the most presti-

gious of performance genres, grand opera, where they get the applause and take the bows while instrumentalists and even the conductor take back seats, stay in the pit until a diva or primo uomo drag
them out to take, looking all embarrassment, a bow with the major
characters. The representatives of nature and pure talent, singers are
a bridge between the everyday population and the skilled instrumentalist who, technique honed to unimaginable degrees, is (like Paga-
nini and Liszt) in league with the devil. We know—and the general
public knows—that singers practice and have a major investment in
technique. But they are closer to average people; anyone can sing a
little, the professionals only do it better. Singers articulate words and
thus keep music closer to everyday experience; they interact with the
audience by gesturing and smiling, something impossible for violinist or organist. And so, to the general public and in the world of
popular music—in contrast to its conception in the professional world
of classical musicians—singing is musical activity of the highest cal-
iber and prestige.

In the Music Building, echoing the view instrumentalists hold of
them, some singers act as if they feel a bit out of place, bewildered,
easily confused, avoiding thorough study of curricular rules, and
generally being—or, more likely, just pretending to be—a bit "out
of it," acting goofy, screaming in the halls, and attacking the unsus-
pecting passer-by by belting out vocalizations, thus perhaps distanc-
ing themselves from the professional norms and showing association
with the general public.

Bowing and Blowing

Hierarchical structure and struggles for hegemony also play a role
among the instruments and instrument families. There is first the
matter of academic primacy: A large number of instruments are taught
and may be presented by a student as his or her major, and these have
long included piano and organ, the modern bowed strings, the woodwinds and trumpet, French horn, and trombone. More recently, tuba,
percussion, and saxophone have been added. A few other instruments
are taught but do not constitute a major in most music schools. Most
prominent of these is the guitar, which is taught as "classical guitar,"
with styles of folk and popular music not included. Other instruments—such as viols or harpsichord for early European music and
certain non-Western instruments—may be taught but for little credit

and no major, while yet another group, including mandolin and banjo, is not represented. The general definition of what *is* taught is "orchestral instruments," and although the designation is not totally correct, the term derives from the central importance of the orchestra in the institution.

In Russia, by contrast, there is an urban-folk analogue to the classical conservatory.[13] There are folk music academies that teach folk instruments (in somewhat modernized and standardized forms) such as the plucked instruments, balalaika and *domra,* and that have orchestras comprised of these instruments in various sizes and pitch levels, whose repertory is largely arrangements and imitations of rural folk songs. The political ideology, avoiding total privileging of classical music, is clear, but the issue does not simply concern egalitarian socialism versus hierarchical capitalism. Issues of ethnicity play a major role in the development of similar or analogous "folk" or indigenous orchestras in Iran, India, and countries of central and Western Europe.

Returning to the range of orchestral instruments in the Heartland, there is a struggle, barely visible on the surface, between winds and strings. In the art music world, the bowed strings represent the quintessence of art. String players are expected to practice a great deal and to eschew other activities; one rarely finds string teachers in administrative positions such as committee chairs, department headships, and deanships. But attendance is best at their concerts, and the audience dresses (well, slightly) better for a string quartet than for a wind quintet concert, to say nothing of a brass ensemble.

The teachers of wind instruments generally (and with important exceptions resulting from individual prestige) receive less respect as musicians and in the purely artistic aspect of their work. This results in part from the repertory of their instruments, which contain fewer works by great masters and less in the way of music from the classical and Romantic periods, the repositories of the greatest music. Instead of representing great art, the wind instruments are associated with music that has, in several senses of the word, political power. Outside the academy, they play "Hail to the Chief," patriotic songs, and marches to honor military victories; their role in governmental ceremonies goes far back in European history. They accompany such acts of patriotism as state funerals or parades. In the university, they are responsible for accompanying major rituals that have a political or even quasi-military component: commencements (chapter 4) and athletic contests, for example, or the governor's ground-breaking ceremonies. The College Music Society makes clear that teachers of wind instruments are also more active than string teachers as committee members and administrators.[14]

Such differences in degree and type of esteem can be ascribed to repertory, because the central works for bowed strings are more closely associated with the great composers of the pantheon, and so the respect violinists and cellists receive as artists is, in part, the prestige of Mozart, Beethoven, Schubert, and Brahms. To some degree, the woodwinds, particularly clarinet and flute, share in this central heritage, but this is less true of brass instruments. The repertorial hierarchy might well be quite different if only twentieth-century music were taken into account, or if it were even given a reasonable proportion of consideration. But the facts that the concertmaster of an orchestra is the first-chair violinist and the ensemble's second-ranking musician (as indicated by such symbols as handshakes with the conductor after concerts) is the first cellist suggest the hegemony of strings in the field of "pure art." The pantheon of late-eighteenth and nineteenth-century masters rules, and musicians and instruments associated with it are artistically in positions of advantage.

Is the Piano King?

If the center of the music school is the group of orchestral instruments and the orchestra itself, the special, and in certain ways dominant, role that the piano plays, orchestral values notwithstanding, may be most clearly emblematic of the Music Building and its culture. In a musical system in which monophony is clearly the exception, the keyboard instruments are the only ones that have substantial solo repertories. The organ, "king of instruments," was not sufficiently mobile and too much associated with religion to become ubiquitous, although many universities and colleges have a special position for a "university organist," harking back to their typically religious association when they were founded. Even so, the piano, associated with the major repertory since the mid-1700s, encapsulates the system on many fronts. It is the only instrument with a large solo repertory whose style fits the expectations of an audience steeped in the Classical and Romantic periods. The normal accompanying instrument, it can play a role in chamber music, is sufficiently powerful to hold its own against an orchestra and thus is the favored vehicle for the concerto genre, and it came to have principal roles in jazz, ragtime, and for long, popular musics. No wonder that the configuration of black and white keys of the keyboard became a principal visual metaphor for classical music.

In the Music Building, the piano plays a perhaps even greater role than in musical life as a whole. In some schools, all curricula require students to become moderately proficient pianists.[15] With the exception of special children's programs such as the Suzuki system of violin teaching, the piano is the only instrument for which class instruction (rather than individual lessons) has been systematically developed. It is the instrument used in theory classes to explain the system of harmony, and students in some schools must take courses in "keyboard harmony" in which they learn to harmonize simple melodies by ear. Graduate programs in musicology and theory, and sometimes in music education, require piano proficiency examinations, including the ability to sight-read, to harmonize, and to play orchestral scores. By the same token, a music school usually has a large number of pianos, providing each faculty member with one in his or her office. If a teacher of virtually any field in music requests a piano, it will normally be provided with much less resistance than other usually less expensive products such as tape recorders or record players. It is taken for granted that a music school must employ one or several technicians to maintain and tune the pianos. At Heartland U. some years ago, the staff included ten full-time piano teachers (plus a few graduate assistants), ten teachers of all types of musicology, six teachers of bowed string instruments, and three full-time piano technicians. The maintenance of the stock of pianos is one of the major financial—and also ideological—commitments of the school.

It is not surprising, therefore, that the piano as instrument and concept has somewhat of a tyrannical component, and that the piano department (and perhaps the piano itself) is regarded as a testing ground, providing hoops to jump through on the way to the degree in a policelike role like that of the theory and musicology departments.

Although an outsider's perspective suggests a number of hierarchies objectively determined, the music school denizens, although agreeing that they live in a hierarchical world, rarely agree on the order in which the school's components are placed on the ladder. Each of the larger groups of performing musicians has a reason for thinking of itself as central or uppermost. The greatest musical art in its most specialized sense is associated with the bowed strings, while teachers and students of vocal art claim superiority on account of the relationship of the voice to the concept of humanity and its closeness to nature; the winds claim musical and academic power on account of their association with political power, while the piano's claim rests on its flexibility and utility. The groups of instruments and the teachers and students associated with them interact in conflict as well as cooperation. But in the end, the metaphor of power rests with the concept of the conducted ensemble and of conducting.

The Importance of Heritage

At a concert of Indian music, the introduction of the musicians by the master of ceremonies or in program notes usually emphasizes the artists' lineages of artistic transmission. There is a recital of the identities of their teachers, perhaps the teachers' own teachers and association with *gharanas,* or schools, of musicianship, and often an attempt to link the main performer of the day through student-teacher genealogies to one of the early great figures of music, such as the revered Tansen, the mythical culture hero and founder of Hindustani music.[16] Elsewhere, the matter of musical descent as a way of providing legitimacy and authority is also emphasized, and it plays a substantial role in Western classical music. It is less the musicians than the audience that must be convinced of the performer's "belonging" to the musical elite in real or simulated biological relationship. Lineage plays a role in the Music Building in two senses, in the identity of your teacher and in your membership in a "musical family."

Whether one is a member of a musical family is only a minor factor in the daily life of the Heartland Music Building. The tendency of Americans to emphasize independence from parents and their desire to be judged on their own accomplishments prevent them from making too much of their musical parents or relatives. And yet in public or formal situations musical genealogy does come up, and this is true of both living students and teachers and of composers and performers of the past. The fact that one is a member of a family of musicians is likely to be noted in a number of ways. There is, for example, always special celebration of the extended family of musical Bachs. Capsule biographies of composers mention musician parents and may note, with a bit of surprise, the absence of known musical personnel in a master's background. Among the living, students at awards ceremonies or banquets are likely to be introduced to friends or at performances with mention of the musical accomplishments, if any, of their parents or other relatives. Attaching entire families to the university ("He represents the third generation of alumni," enthuses the chief of fund-raising) plays a special role in the music school. This concept of musical families plays more of a role in American society than that of families of businessmen, physicians, or scientists. The imbalance may have to do with the concept of talent, thought to have genetic components and associated more with music than with these other fields (one rarely hears that a person is a "talented physician"). It may be connected to the notion of the musicians as cultural outsiders, a society of their own.

More important in the social structure of musicians than the biological family is the familylike unit comprised of teacher and students. In music school, such a unit is often called a "studio," referring to the room in which a teacher gives lessons. The vita of a musician, teacher, or student emphasizes a listing of "with whom" that person has studied as a major qualification, and this is true even if the course of study was brief or not very successful. As at Indian concerts, this genealogy may also be presented in program notes.

Certain lineages became particularly important in twentieth-century Europe and the Americas, their social (although probably not musical) role paralleling that of the Indian *gharanas*. One of the most famous centers on Theodor Leschetitzky (1830–1915), who claimed authority because he had been a student of Carl Czerny (1771–1857), a personal student of Beethoven's. Leschetitzky was a very successful teacher and could count among his students such greats as I. Paderewski, O. Gabrilowitsch, and A. Schnabel, as well as a large number of far less distinguished pupils.[17] During the 1930s and 1940s, many claimed to have been his students, and membership in that group might give one a few additional points at musicians' cocktail parties. Indeed, after his death a large Leschetitzky Society was established, with branches in Europe and the United States, to which only his personal students were admitted.

If the Beethoven heritage—for obvious reasons—played a major role, that of Franz Liszt became equally prominent. One of his famous and influential students was Moritz Rosenthal, whose student, Ernst Hofzimmer, became a piano professor at a Heartland school and produced many piano teachers who thus trace themselves back to the heritage of Liszt. In the middle 1940s, Hofzimmer was letting his hair grow and otherwise affecting a Lisztian manner of appearance, and, insisting on certain practicing procedures, he referred off and on to Rosenthal. In a somewhat similar fashion, many violinists of the first half of the twentieth century, European and American, prided themselves in having been students of Leopold Auer (1845–1930), who was primarily known as a pedagogue and counted Mischa Elman, Efrem Zimbalist, and Jascha Heifetz among his students and also included many much lesser-known players and teachers who through their association with Auer brought themselves closer to Elman and Heifetz. Later, Ivan Galamian (b. 1902) assumed the role of principal teacher of many prominent violinists, among them Pinchas Zukerman, Jaime Laredo, Itzhak Perlman, Paul Zukofsky, and Michael Rabin.[18]

These teachers were not famed as performers but as pedagogues; the substantive value of their instruction is beyond dispute. But a "school"—the group of students and perhaps their students as well—of such a teacher, once established, confers credit and esteem on its members. It is distinguished by particular approaches to music and technique. To be able to claim to have been a student of a great teacher gives evidence of talent as recognized by an authority. Having been good enough, or promising enough, to be accepted by a particular teacher may in itself provide evidence of your qualifications. In the world of art music, the identity of the teacher and membership in a school often play at least a marginal role in a student's career, quite apart from the substantive value of a famous teacher's instruction.

The concept of schools and the identity of one's teacher play a significant role in other parts of Western society. In conventional American academic life, its counterpart is the university or college or department. Scholars of humanistic disciplines or social sciences are known to some extent by their principal teachers, especially by the advisors of their dissertation work. More typically, they are associated with departments and universities. Thus, at the point at which a pianist is introduced before a recital as student of the famous Maestro X, a lecturer in history or anthropology is introduced as "a graduate of Harvard" or as one who "received his Ph.D. at Northwestern." The solidarity of students and alumni of a studio are somewhat like the solidarity of the alumni of a department of musicology.[19]

Within the social structure of the Music Building, the concept of "studio" is much more personalized than that of "department."[20] A student identifies himself or herself as belonging to a particular teacher's studio. At award ceremonies, and even in student recitals, performers are usually identified as "student of Professor X," who may also share in the glory of an award by being the presenter or, rarely, the corecipient. In contrast to academic life in general, in which a student takes courses with many teachers and may have different advisors for senior, master's, and doctor's theses, a student of voice or instruments commonly remains with one teacher throughout her or his course of study at one university. Often there is no choice; the Music Building is likely to have only one organ, oboe, trombone, or viola teacher, but in such cases the identity of the teacher is likely to determine which music school or department a student will select.

But in departments of voice, piano, or violin, where there is likely to be a faculty of a half dozen, the choice of whom to study with and whom to teach makes a major difference. There is a certain amount of competition for the best (or most famous, or most influential) professors, and teachers in turn vie for the most talented students. Conflicts are resolved by division chairs or deans, and, as in the case of conducting, the bestowing of talented students on teachers is part of the system of rewards.

Once they become members of a teacher's studio, students are generally expected to show loyalty to the teachers by attending their recitals, helping as page-turners, publicizing the teacher's accomplishments, and celebrating birthdays and successes. Teachers, in turn, are likely to favor their own students over those of other faculty members by helping them get engagements and jobs, or when grading by juries takes place. All together, however, the studios of different teachers—the group of teachers each with his or her group of major students—constitute a hierarchy. An incoming student may therefore be eager to join the studio of a highly reputed teacher not only because of the teacher's excellence and fame, but also in order to be associated with the supposedly excellent group of students who have gathered around the teacher. Whether a freshman upon arrival has been assigned to Violin Teacher I, a full professor who concertizes internationally; or Violin Teacher II, a junior faculty member who is promising but not famous; or Violin Teacher III, an older faculty member who never played widely and is regarded as an inferior teacher and whose retirement is being avidly awaited—all make a great difference in a student's career. The assignment is important because it indicates the faculty's appraisal of the student's talent, that elusive concept that can only be properly evaluated in retrospect after it has been developed, but whose initial appraisal is a major determinant of success.

This procedure is all taken for granted by the denizens of the Music Building. The fame and prestige of teachers and the talents of students always play a role in academic life, but departments other than those of the arts, such as history or anthropology, tend to divide students and teachers more in accordance with subject specialization. There, the most famous senior faculty may be eschewed as thesis advisors by certain graduate students because they may be expected to be too demanding, intimidating, and inattentive. Thus the tendency on the part of graduate students in traditional academic disciplines is often to seek out teachers and research advisors who are younger but sympathetic. In the minds of students of performance and of music deans, however, teachers are definitely ranked, and a student's first choice, normally, is to study with the "first chair."

A Group of Ensembles

The Social Role of Performing Groups

Some members of Heartland society view a music school as basically a building; to others, it may be a group of professors, a body of students, or a set of courses and a curriculum. But many people in the music-loving academic public appear to see the university community fundamentally as a group of performing ensembles. These are the emblems by which the school is recognized. The centrality of ensembles, and of the purpose of the music school as the provider of essential ceremonial services, were already recognized at the University of Illinois by 1914, when the university's president, offering the position of director of the music school, made it clear that the incumbent's principal duty would be to provide performances much more than it would be to teach or administer the work of other teachers.

> The Director would be expected to be responsible for the conduct of the school in every respect. He has also general supervision of the musical interests of the university. He is expected to

develop and maintain a choral society, see that an efficient orchestra is kept in valuable operation. . . .

He would be expected to see that public recitals are given by pupils of the musical school and by members of the faculty of the music school and that such other concerts should be organized and given as circumstances may make feasible. . . .

. . . you would be expected to furnish music for all public occasions, either in the form of quartette, octette, or solo singing by students or professors, or organ, or orchestral productions, or the band. Whatever you can get your colleagues to do is so much in your favor. In the last analysis, if you can not get them to do a thing you must do it yourself.[21]

Even now, colleges and universities that have no music department normally maintain choruses, orchestras, and bands; some music departments were originally organized around such groups. The role of these ensembles within a music school is primarily educational; even more, they are part of the entertainment arm of the university, a role they share with departments of theater, dance, and fine arts, with lecture series, and with athletics.

Going to college is intended to be an education, but it turns out to be a way of life. The university provides for virtually all needs of a student, and education is not confined to classroom and courses. The university provides a large number of optional activities that combine education with entertainment. Included here are plays, concerts, lectures, athletic events, museums, and the library insofar as it is used for recreational reading. These all could be placed in various continuums and in two categories—those for which one must buy tickets and those that are free. The paid ones include football games, concerts, opera, theater, and dance performances; lectures, university museums, and the library are free.

We take all this for granted, professors readily admitting that students almost feel that they should get paid, rather than pay, for attending lectures, and the notion of charging a dollar for borrowing an unassigned book seems totally off the wall. Such a hypothetical system is quite conceivable. The point is that certain of these educational and entertainment activities are regarded as relatively frivolous and therefore should be paid for by consumers, whereas others are more purely educational and, imposing an earlier value, serious and edifying. They should, therefore, be free.

Concerts, including the concerts of the student ensembles them-selves (to say nothing of those by distinguished visiting musicians), normally require tickets at some institutions. In the performing arts center of one Heartland school, even recitals by professors (themselves not paid explicitly for the performances) in 1992 cost students $1 and others $3; the same was true of concerts by the student orchestra. But when lectures take place in these same halls, no tickets are needed. No matter that hearing concerts plays a role in a music student's education rather like that of reading literature in the training of an English major. Music is, to a large degree, classed within the frivo-lous sector of the campus's entertainment world. To be sure, distinc-tions are made, even within the gamut of musical performances. For operas (the most frivolous, or at any rate the most secular and the most hierarchical of music performances), one must buy expensive tickets. For organ concerts (the most serious, most associated with religion, and, as I endeavor to show in chapter 4, containing much music that is less hierarchical), one rarely buys tickets. Confronted with the discrepancy, the administration gives as the reason the high cost of producing operas and the location of the organ (in a hall where tickets are ordinarily not sold or in a church), ignoring the enormous installation and maintenance costs of organs.

The ensembles of the music school exist, in good part, to pro-vide entertainment for the local community; their noneducational component is symbolized by the fact that one must buy tickets to attend the performances. The number of ensembles in music schools is considerable, numbering from twenty to upward of forty, the ma-jority of them explicitly conducted by faculty members. This list does not include chamber groups such as string quartets and piano trios, although borderline cases (as with the role of conductor) such as African mbira or xylophone or advanced jazz ensembles may be listed. Each ensemble has a special purpose in terms of repertory, level of excellence, and prestige. Here is the list from a large school during a representative semester: (1) university orchestra; (2) cham-ber orchestra; (3) collegium musicum; (4) string ensemble; (5) woodwind ensemble; (6) brass ensemble; (7) percussion ensemble; (8) oratorio society (community chorus); (9) university chorus; (10) women's chorus; (11) black chorus; (12) women's glee club; (13) men's glee club; (14) concert choir; (15) opera theater; (16–19) jazz band (four); (20) harp ensemble; (21) piano ensemble; (22) madrigal singers; (23) wind ensemble; (24–25) symphonic bands 1 and 2; (26–27) second concert bands A and B; (28) marching band; (29) brass band; (30) clarinet choir; (31) contemporary ensemble; (32) improvisation ensemble; (33) university chorale; (34) advanced jazz ensemble; (35) advanced wind ensemble; (36) advanced orchestral ensemble; (37) Baroque ensemble; (38) contemporary chamber singers; (39) gamelan; (40) African drum ensemble; and (41) East African mbira ensemble.

Allowing for some overlapping of designations in order to permit graduate and undergraduate students to perform together, about thirty separate ensembles require a leader or conductor. Why so many? Administrators may say that they are needed because students want to make music together, and the opportunity to do so is an important part of education. "We must make our faculty and facilities available for the maintenance of these ensembles because our students need to play in them as an essential part of their training" is a typical way of putting it.

The Power of the Baton

In addition to educational and entertainment functions, ensembles play a major part in the way power relationships function among the three classes inhabiting the Music Building. This chapter began with a consideration of sociomusical classes in the Music Building, classes distinguished by considerations of activity, function, and time. I then described some of the other—principally musical—ways in which denizens of the Music Building group themselves by instrument type, degree of commitment to performance, association with teachers, and, eventually, performing group. To associate the social, socioeconomic, and musical structures, one must discuss and relate the two central bases of power in the music school: the office of dean, or head, or director, and the conductor's baton. To do so, it is necessary to return to the significance of chronology in careers, for as the norm for a music academic is to rise from student to professor to dean, the ultimate goal of a typical classical musician is to conduct.

Almost everyone (and that includes some who would deny it) wants to conduct, and this includes deans and professors. It's the goal of a majority of successful performers, of composers, and even sometimes of scholars and educators in classical music, the ultimate power trip. One of the important facts about ensembles in the music school is that ordinarily all performers are students, whereas conductors are almost always teachers. This relationship supports the significance of the class distinction between students and faculty, or faculty and administrators, and the homology of power relations in politics and education. It also leads to the suggestion that the large ensemble in the music world is the model for the social organization of the Music Building.

One normal path to conducting in the nonacademic music world is to excel as an instrumentalist and, in the case of choral music, perhaps as a singer, but instrumentalists sometimes become choral conductors, whereas singers virtually never become orchestra conductors. Fine violinists (such as Zubin Mehta) and cellists (such as Arturo Toscanini) come to mind, and even unusually outstanding instrumentalists such as Mstislav Rostropovich, Alexander Schneider, and Pablo Casals moved into conducting late in their careers. Composers sometimes turn to conducting (for example, Gustav Mahler and Pierre Boulez), and some individuals, such as Bruno Walter and Fritz Reiner, evidently set out to be conductors early in their careers.[22]

One path to the musician's ideal of conducting, however, is to become a university teacher, the kind of job in which one can virtually count on getting the opportunity to conduct an ensemble. *Count on* may be too positive a term, and yet at Heartland U. twenty-six of eighty teachers were engaged in conducting something in some way during a single semester. At the same time, students, whose task it is to learn the skills of conducting they will need as teachers and otherwise (at most schools, one course in conducting is required), engage in conducting the school's ensembles in public quite rarely.

One of the most characteristic features of music schools that arises as a point of abiding controversy over the decades is the "ensemble requirement." The music school's official position is that ensembles are created in order to provide much-needed opportunities for students to learn repertory and techniques of musical cooperation. It is for this reason that each undergraduate, and in some cases each graduate, student is required to perform in an ensemble during each semester of enrollment. From the viewpoint of learning repertory and technique, the requirement is rational. It is reasonable also because the school needs to provide music for ceremonies and as entertainment, and it is difficult to staff these ensembles with unpaid musicians in the absence of a requirement. But a third contributing cause is the value of the concept of conducting as a demonstration of power.

What is usually required of students is participation in "conduct-ed" ensembles—eliminating chamber combinations such as string quartets or small jazz combos despite the fact that the art music world's central repertory between 1730 and 1920 includes a great deal of music for chamber groups or small ensembles appropriate as materi-al for music and academic requirements. It seems to me that the val-ue of conducting is at least partially involved.

Officially, each student must perform in one ensemble, but in practice many students join several, and some complain about pres-sure to join not just the required one, but six or eight. Matters of repertory and genre surely play a role, and also—to put it perhaps more crudely than is appropriate—some professors may create en-sembles in order to provide themselves with the opportunity of con-ducting. As teachers and those responsible for dispensing scholarship and awards, they may be able to put pressure on excellent student performers to join their ensembles.

As conductors, professors receive the satisfaction of leadership in rehearsals (it is actually a dictatorial leadership that does not readily permit advice and consent) and also the glory that goes with public performance in which the conductor emerges as a member of a rul-ing class, receiving vastly more credit for the performance than the individual ensemble member. All of the school's ensembles work to-ward the presentation of public performances at least once a semes-ter, thus becoming part of the university's entertainment arm and contributing to the public view of the music school as principally a group of performing ensembles.

There is a dual set of relationships between the class structure of the music school and the concept of the ensemble in Western art music, between music school administrators and conductors as fact and concept. The professorial conductor of an ensemble is "dean for an hour," or deans or heads may sometimes act like conductors. In most universities, department heads or deans carry out teaching and research along with administration, remain heads temporarily, and work within an essentially democratic structure. In colleges of liber-al arts, deans may be professors of sociology, history, or French and do not use, or perhaps have, a role model from the outside world. The dean who comes from sociology does not act like a government official in the Department of Health and Human Services, and the French professor/dean does not imitate Jean-Paul Sartre. The head of the art school does not have the model of the Renaissance paint-er-cum-workshop director in mind, but in music the parallel is obviously available. The typical music school head who has decided to "go into administration" has risen from the labor force, expects never to return, and is likely to carry out the task with the techniques of a benevolent dictator. The number of music school administrators who move on into general university administration at the highest levels is remarkable.

Music school teachers are generally inclined to accept a rather paternalistic style of administration, as musicians accept the dictatorship of the conductor. As evidence I cite their tendency to elect their department heads to other kinds of positions of responsibility, such as general university committees and membership on governing boards of professional societies. Except for cases of egregious abuse, they seem to accept the class structure and the "strong dean" system. It is probably not coincidental that the music school at Heartland U. was one of the last academic units to write bylaws for its governance.

If the model for music school administration is the role of the conductor and the power and prestige it presents, one result is that conductorships are sought after even more avidly in music schools than in the world of music at large. Being "given" an ensemble to direct is usually cause for congratulation—more than being assigned a new, interesting course; it is at the very least an indication of confidence. Professors who have been offered positions at other institutions are encouraged to stay on by a number of conventional means that include salary raises, promotions in rank, and promises of leaves for research; for musicians, the promise of a conducting spot may also be included. Furthermore, a faculty member in a position perceived as disadvantageous may make up for lost status by conducting an ensemble. At Heartland U., the second violinist in a resident string quartet became the conductor of the orchestra, and a professor of percussion, once an inferior position in the art music world, considered it very important to become conductor of the new music ensemble.

There is no doubt that women are disproportionately unrepresented among music school heads and as conductors. The same is true, perhaps to an even a greater extent, for African Americans and other members of minorities. But the situation is changing. In the 1950s, one could hardly conceive of women as candidates for deanships of large schools of music. That they were sometimes chairs of small music departments is a relic of the time when the teaching of music itself was regarded as a woman's profession. Anecdotal evidence suggests that these female administrators tended to be personally imposing. Female conductors are still rare, more common in the choral field than in the orchestral and rarest in bands. The system of classes that culminates in deaning or conducting is affected by the general American tradition of discrimination against women and members of minorities.

The bestowing of conductorships on professors is a prerogative of the head or dean. Conducting is basically a position of power; in a sense, conductors are not the specialized technicians that instrumentalists and composers must be. Virtually all conductors are also—or were originally—something else. Thus, instrumentalists, composers, even vocalists and sometimes also musicologists tend to feel qualified to conduct. Although there are, of course, good and bad conductors, the music world tends to select them on the basis of their prestige as instrumentalists or composers. In the academic music world, it is sometimes less the ability to play or compose and more one's influence and general prestige, one's political power, that determines whether one will conduct. And so, the music dean may reward professors by "giving" them ensembles, and in doing so turns over a kind of miniature deanship.[23]

It may seem logical to university administrators and music faculties to look to conductors as the natural academic leaders of music schools. If a conductor can be "a dean for an hour," that conductor may also become the dean for good. The directory of music departments and schools published by the College Music Society reveals a somewhat disproportionate number of conductors who are department heads.[24] About 13 percent of faculty members are listed as conductors of ensembles in their departments (this includes small departments with very few ensembles), but about 25 percent of department heads are listed as regular conductors.

It would seem that faculty and perhaps the higher administration of the university perceive a homology between musical and academic administration. Becoming a conductor is as much a matter of having a group of musicians whom one can conduct as of technical ability, so administrators have the prerogative of designating a conductor and may designate themselves. There may well be substantive reasons; a conductor must have some administrative talent to manage the job and also some charisma of leadership, and music faculties may want to be led by a person who can lead not only the department but also the music. The parallel is clear and significant to all concerned. Conducting, the most elevated of musical positions, and administration, the most elevated academically, are lines of work for which specialized training is often not available and not necessarily expected. In any event, there is no coherent tradition of teaching and practicing as there is for instrumentalists and vocalists, or of teachers and scholars.

It is tempting also to see what other kinds of faculty members often become heads of music departments and to speculate about the reasons. Frequently (but this has been true only since about 1970) they are musicologists, and perhaps this has occurred because musicologists tend to have the highest earned degrees in music departments and, more than other musicians, have had training and experience parallel to that of the more typical academics, with whom they communicate easily. Department heads are also frequently composers, the producers of music in the most central sense; they are often also teachers of music education, whose curricula sometimes include courses in the administration of music departments. A good many department heads or deans are teachers of performance (or "applied music," as it is called in music school jargon). Among them, teachers of wind instruments are often department heads. Pianists, organists, vocalists, and, most notably, string teachers are rarely found. The greater frequency of wind players may have to do with the association of wind instruments with ritual and political power in Western culture. Thus, it appears that the relationships of art and ritual, of art and political power, play a role in the selection of music school administrators.

The complex, and perhaps Byzantine, social and sociomusical organization of music schools results from a combination of factors: the transfer of the industrial model of corporations and markets to an educational environment; the role of music in Western and particularly American society, again transferred to the academic framework; the symbolic roles of various instruments, of singing and conducting and their relationship to the roles of various groups in society; the hegemony of large musical ensembles as musical metaphors of large, successful organizations in which each member plays a specialized part; the imposition of the taxonomy of races and genders on the musical and educational scene; the concept of talent and its presumption from a musician's association with others, living or dead; the concept of genius, associated with a pantheon of composers no longer living; and the willingness of musicians in art music society to play with relationships in ways reminiscent of political and social processes that might not be readily accepted in other domains of the culture of modern real-life America.

~ 3 ~

A Place for All Musics?
Confrontation and Mediation

A Meeting Place

Center and Periphery

"Good" Music and the Rest. The institutions I have been discussing are officially named "School of Music" or "Department of Music," but they are clearly not devoted to the study, and certainly not to the advocacy, of all music. They are, it has been clear all along, schools of Western European art music, but the visiting E.T. ethnomusicologist must be startled to find that, when other musics are included at all, it is only on special terms. Even the various sorts of Western art music may not be included on equal terms. Actually, there are some ways in which the music school functions almost as an institution for the suppression of certain musics. Its library may avoid the purchase of popular music, and in decades past some music deans forbade students to play popular music or jazz in their spare time; even now, some voice teachers discourage their students from singing jazz or non-Western music because it might harm their voices.

The selection of canons of words or materials appropriate for study has been an issue in higher education forever, and certainly in recent years. For a long time, the inclusion of "popular history" in the curricula of history departments, commercial art in art history, or even the culture of mestizo communities in anthropology departments devoted to pure cultures was greeted with ambivalence. We are told that intrinsic quality and significance (of person, event, work) determine inclusion. Whether history is the deeds of great people, the interaction of impersonal movements, or the description of changes in everyday life is an abiding issue for teachers of history. But in the selection of canons, there is a qualitative difference between these other disciplines. Criticizing a student for reading about a decade in a Balkan village instead of the battles of Napoleon, a history teacher might tell her that she is wasting her time. But some teachers of music history would accuse students who listen to Elvis Presley not only of taking time away from hearing Brahms, but also of polluting themselves. In its judgment of the interrelationships of musics in its community, the music school is very much concerned with the concept of pollution. Some of the energy of the Heartland music school, at least before the late 1980s, was devoted to protecting students from bad music and promulgating what is often labeled as "serious" music (or seriously called "good music") or, not so facetiously, "real" music.[1]

To be sure, one may be told that in each kind of music—classical, jazz, Indian, African—there may be both good and bad. One sometimes may hear self-satisfied statements, ascribed apocryphally to various composers, to the effect that there are only two kinds of music, good and bad. But the fact that some radio stations specializing in Western art music call themselves "good music stations" indicates the classical establishment's general attitude. The ranking of musics and the avoidance of pollution of the good music and its performers by the others—by avoidance or what might be compared to purification rituals—are important components of music school life.

Two kinds of purification ritual come to mind: (1) the performance of music in—hopefully—complete accord with the composer's "intentions," on authentic instruments and with authoritative performance practice; and (2) the performance of all works by a composer or of a composer's works for a particular medium, as, for example, a series of concerts giving all of Beethoven's string quartets, all of Schubert's more than six hundred lieder (something done at one Heartland university over a period of six years), or all of Mozart's works in one season.

A canon may be variously shaped. In the system of musical education, it may consist of a limited number of works, or of all works by a group of exalted composers, or even of a specified group of genres or styles. Boundaries may be definite or vague, narrow or wide. But in the Music Building people talk about works, not performances, about composers, not performers.[2] The various approaches to establishing canons in Western art music always revolve around the music work as a fundamental unit.

Concentric Circles. One way to comprehend the taxonomy and relative value of musics in the Music Building is to use the concept of concentric circles (the canon at the center). This structure describes both the relationship of repertories and an important aspect of social organization of the school.

The center is classical Western music (almost exclusively European music) composed roughly between 1720 and 1930. There is no single accepted term that represents this sector of art music, but the music community often uses *common-practice music* or *standard music.* I would suggest the term *central repertory.* It is what the music school considers music par excellence, as suggested by the way in which the library treats it in the scheme of subject headings or the institution in its curricular catalogs and schedules.

Outside the central repertory, special designations are needed because there are courses on "jazz," "folk music," "popular music," and "ethnic music." The terms *early music* and *contemporary music* are used to separate the "normal" music from others in the art music sphere. It is implied that "normal music" (even in North America) means European music, whereas other kinds of music, both in the college and the library catalogs, are labeled by nation or area: "American music," "music—India," and "Indians of North America—music," for example. There is also a group of specialties whose style is in the realm of "real" music but are treated as somewhat outside its scope: women's music (by female composers but perhaps also for functions associated with women), American music, Latin American art music, and percussion music. These may be peripheral because their repertories include some material in styles outside the central. On social occasions, these musics require special attention, and their existence sometimes raises a bit of humor.

The various musics that are not "central" have had to struggle over a period of decades for entry into the music school. They usually gained admission via the back door of musicology because faculty and administrators felt, on first application, that one should not teach them as fields of performance, but that it might be all right to teach "about" them because they could be helpful in fostering an understanding of the evolution of the central repertory or of the cultures of early, recent, contemporary, foreign, or rural peoples.[3] Even now, when they are included in the performing curricula, these musics (and they include early and new musics) are usually included in such nonperforming departments as musicology, ethnomusicology, and composition that take care, respectively, of the study of performance of early, non-Western, and new music.

Yet the non-central musics have taken their places in the music school, although the management of the music school, the administration, usually makes clear its allegiance to the central music. It is unusual, for example, for administrators to have musical roots that are not in the central music. Some do come from fields such as ethnomusicology or composition (viewed with some suspicion by the performing faculty), but in each case, some kind of loyalty, in terms of early training or avocation, to the "real" music is characteristic in the administrator. The most radical of composers or ethnomusicologists have very rarely become administrators. Deans or directors who conduct large ensembles confine themselves primarily to repertory from the central music era. Those associated with a peripheral music avoid public performance. In choosing events to attend, deans or heads usually prefer central-repertory performances over performances of peripheral music or nonmusical events such as lectures.

The social organization of the music school is related in several ways to the coexistence and interrelationship of several musical styles and repertories in these institutions. Social groups correlate with repertories: A teacher's or a student's personal associations within the school are determined in part by the musical repertory with which he or she is identified. Performers and audiences deal with classes, types, and genres of music as if they were a society reflecting the society of humans (chapter 4). Musics (and submusics, if you will) are related on the basis of musical values—complexity, relationship to the central repertory, and innovativeness—as well as by nationality and social class. It is instructive to consider the schools of music at large American universities as places where many musics converge and collide, as do cultures on a broader scale. Common-practice music is clearly at the center of instruction, theory, and the concert scene and is surrounded by other art music, with most non-Western and popular music further on, at the periphery. Yet it is appropriate to regard music schools as fundamentally polymusical organizations in which many musics meet and interact, maintaining far more contact than in other cultural venues in the American Heartland and, for that matter, elsewhere in the United States and Europe.

A Bit of Recent History. Polymusicality has not always been the rule; the world of musics in music schools of 1950 was substantially different and determinedly unimusical. Despite the fact that many schools were not all that much smaller than they are now, teachers and students devoted themselves almost completely to the study and propagation of the central classical music. There was, to be sure, some interest in "new" music, with composers such as Schoenberg, Bartók, Hindemith, and Copland at the cutting edge, but the tendency was not to regard this recent music as a distinct, new language, but to integrate it into the musical and sociocultural framework of the classical, incorporated into the central performance framework and repertory. Thus, works of Bartók, Stravinsky, and Webern were occasionally performed concerts along with earlier music. (It is interesting to compare the special concerts of new music sponsored by organizations such as the American Society for Contemporary Music that were held in the public music world of cities such as New York.) The idea at Heartland music schools around 1950 was not to establish a separate category of new music for a newly established musical language, but to expand the scope of the central classic concept.

Early (pre-1650) music was rarely performed in 1950 except as a music history or theory classroom exercise, and there were no concerts of non-Western or ethnic music and no folk music performances beyond the few that took place outside the school of music and were sponsored by and located in other units of the university. Jazz was barely beginning to make inroads, only on the assumption that it could somehow be integrated into the classical framework with the use of the large band and conductor, printed music, and little improvisation. The unimusical conception of the school was not questioned, and suggestions that one might introduce musics outside the central classical into the concert schedule or the curriculum were greeted as jokes. Music education and appreciation courses concentrated almost totally on the so-called common-practice styles. Theory courses were almost exclusively devoted to functional harmony along with sixteenth-century counterpoint.[4]

In contrast to the more multicultural leanings of departments of visual art, which were already offering courses on Far Eastern and African art, the Heartland music school of the 1950s accepted the central classical repertory as the proper music of the culture and the institution. Other music was kept away; it was ignored, relegated in courses to special short bits somehow to underscore its inappropriateness, and kept out of the lives of students through administrative discouragement. It was not an institution in which musical cultures met. Forty years later, the midwestern university school of music, substantially increased in size through economic prosperity and population growth, had become one of the institutions in American society in which musics do indeed meet. But it is an institution that makes judgments about the ways in which these musics, and the societies they reflect, may relate to each other.

The World of Musics, Bimusicality and Polymusicality. Musicologists (including ethnomusicologists) have typically seen the musical world as a group of discrete musics, each of which has a structure, provenance, and relationship to a society somewhat like that of a language. A society is, after all, a group of people with a distinct culture, usually a language as well, the kind of unit that is colloquially called an "ethnic group" or "nationality." The guiding basic assumption in ethnomusicology is that a society has *a* music, or at least a principal music, that consists of a set of rules and principles that govern ideas about music, musical behavior, and musical sound and is comprised of a repertory of some degree of consistency and a hierarchy of central and peripheral phenomena. There is Italian music, Chinese music, Arapaho music, and Ewe music. This congruence of society and music is certainly an oversimplification and readily subject to criticism from several perspectives, but it is a point of departure. It is important to admit with Slobin that membership in individual musical cultures has become more a matter of interest and competence than of ethnic identity.[5] Yet the individual musics, even if not congruent with societies or subcultures, are maintained as distinct units in the taxonomy of American academic life.

Building on the analogy with language, bimusicality and polymusicality play a greater and more complicated role in musical culture than their linguistic counterparts. Although competence in a language can be established more or less easily, it is difficult to determine just what is required for a person to "have competence in," participate in, "understand," possess, or "identify with" a music. Languages are moderately close to equal in complexity and amount of content, such as size of vocabulary. However musics differ greatly, at least in quantity, length of units (pieces, songs), and number of desirable timbres such as instruments, variety of available textures, and, most of all, size of repertory. Beyond that, a polymusical person may participate in a variety of musics to very different degrees and in very different ways.

Assuming that a large and complex society such as that of the United States has a considerable number of musics, we can imagine a variety of acceptable degrees of individual competence. For example, a professional clarinetist might play in a symphony orchestra and teach clarinet (her main music is "central classical"), occasionally sit in a jazz ensemble but not considered excellent, try to listen occasionally to records of rock music in order to empathize with her teenage son, once have taken a course in Indian music, and occasionally try to play classical songs from Madras on her instrument. This clarinetist participated in a tour of Peru, where she heard a good deal of Quechua and Aymara music and liked it, and she plays but generally dislikes (and claims not to understand) some works of post-1960 new music. How polymusical is this musician? Her musical life too could be described as a set of concentric circles, with Western classical music in the center. We can imagine analogous situations in linguistic participation, but the complex kind of musical life just described is probably quite common in American culture and would not readily find its analogue in language behavior.

A Blackfoot man whom I knew claimed to have two musics central in his life—the intertribal powwow repertory of Plains Indian cultures and the country and western music that he plays in a small band in a bar. He was also trying to learn, but slowly, some older and explicitly Blackfoot ceremonial music. He played trumpet in high school band and learned the typical repertory of such institutions (marches and some concert band music), he goes to a Methodist church and can sing several hymns from memory, and—a person of some curiosity—he has seen two opera or musical comedy productions at a nearby college. Such a structure, with dual center, shares characteristics with the concentric circle format and may often be found among members of American minorities.

This type of musical persona has become increasingly the norm in the cultures of the world. Slobin suggests that the musical culture of the West consists, at least in the second half of the twentieth century, of a series of what he calls "micromusics," interacting units somewhat equivalent to the "musics" in this chapter and the musics Finnegan views as coexisting in a small, relatively homogeneous community.[6] In each analysis, the typical individual is multimusical. If ever there were a time when the typical individual in most societies had access only to a single music, the music of the homogeneous culture, the situation is now virtually the opposite. But if individuals are now frequently polymusical, the institutions and contexts for musical performance in which they participate may be either unimusical or polymusical. The following are all examples of institutions that are principally unimusical: the Blackfoot powwow; the Metropolitan Opera House; the First Lutheran Church; the club of eight or ten middle-class men in North Tehran devoted to Persian classical music; Sastri Hall, home of Carnatic concerts, in the Mylapore district of Madras; the Rose Bowl bar in Urbana, Illinois (home of country music of the 1950s); the typical American radio station devoted to jazz, heavy metal, 1960s' rock, rap, church music, or classical music; and conceivably even the violin lesson or the rehearsal of the big-band jazz organization. (I have not heard of teachers of classical violin music, including country and western, jazz, or Carnatic violin, playing in their lesson plans.)

Mediators

If musical organizations and institutions typically exist for the propagation of one music, there are also those whose function, and sometimes purpose, is to effect mediation among musics. In the music histories of some societies, such units—concerts, recordings, and music schools—seem in the last several decades to have increased gradually in significance.

Concerts. The public concert in Europe gradually (and no doubt with exceptions, detours, and reverses) moved from the presentation of music in one style, or by one composer, to something requiring diversity and synthesis. Many concerts around 1820 in West European cities consisted of music from the present and the immediate past (e.g., a concert of a variety of works by Beethoven).[7] Today, representative orchestra concerts include music from a span of two hundred years, and many choral concerts provide material from the early seventeenth century to the late twentieth. Even so, these concerts are not mediators among musics in the larger sense; they still include only central art music. They may, however, provide a mix of materials that might at one time have been perceived as incompatible.

The introduction of the public, Western-style concert in other societies had a similar effect in more emphatic form. The concerts of Carnatic music that take place in Madras during the afternoons and evenings of the "music season," in December and early January, consist of songs and improvisations in all sorts of ragas, some of them traditionally winter or summer ragas, or morning and evening ragas, all at the same time and season and in new sorts of juxtapositions. Or again, a traditional Persian performance, most frequently taking place in private venue, would consist of a lengthy exposition of a single *dastgah* (mode), but modern public concerts, given in concert halls during the evening and complete with printed programs and intermissions, would provide short performances of four or five *dastgahs*. Or, going further afield in synthesis and combination, a concert by the American Indian Dance Theater combines many kinds of Indian music and dance—material from different cultural areas, from different times, and with varying degrees of fantasy and Westernization. Thus, a concert itself may be seen as a mediating institution among musical cultures. Nevertheless, in Heartland music schools, concerts keep musics separate rather than providing synthesis.

Recordings. The existence and ready availability of recordings has broadened the musical experience of many millions of individuals, making private homes venues for the meeting of musical cultures. But record stores are actually more obvious mediating locales in North America as well as in Indian cities, and even on Native American reservations. The typical record store sells music of various sorts. In a record store in Tehran around 1970 one would have found (in separate sections) Iranian popular music; Western popular music; some (admittedly little) music from India, Afghanistan, and Arabic nations; some Persian classical music; Islamic sermons and Koran readings; and Western classical music. In Madras, a city in which patrons of live performance concentrated on Carnatic music and some film music performed in night clubs, certain record stores would also have carried Hindustani music, a large quantity of film music in various languages and from various parts of India, and a small amount of music from outside India.[8]

American record stores have separate sections: rock, pop, soul, rhythm and blues, country, folk, classical, and "international." On Indian reservations, stores selling records—usually those that also sell other kinds of specifically Indian artifacts—provide recordings of music by a variety of Indian peoples, in a number of styles and with various degrees of modernization, and music in totally Western styles performed by Indians. There seems to be no literature about the ways in which record store patrons interact in stores and to what extent they are stimulated to permit different musics to meet in their experience, but these shops at least provide the opportunity for musical cultures to meet.[9]

Finally, Music Schools. There are other mediating institutions: certain films and film music traditions (for example, the multistylistic film repertory of the Indian film industry), radio stations (but not the typical American music stations, which specialize in narrow repertories), libraries, festivals, and central locations such as certain city squares or, more recently, performing arts centers.[10] A Heartland university school of music in the period from 1980 to 1990 was also among the institutions that mediated among many musics by welcoming a number of distinct kinds into its scope of activity; by providing a taxonomy for them and permitting them to interact; and finally by providing roles and functions for them and their adherents to present them in a hierarchy and suggest ways in which the highest may be served by the others.

A Taxonomy of Concerts

In trying to justify the description of the music school as an institution whose denizens think of it as populated by different musics, and establishing the boundaries among them, the ethnomusicologist from Mars is bound to ask whether the somewhat vague and broad taxonomy based on aspects of style and sound, common to the terminology of the school's citizens, is reflected elsewhere. One kind of answer comes from examining aspects of the concert that do not involve musical sound at all, such as the performers' costumes and interactions with each other and the audience. I have touched on the issue of costumes earlier by saying that "clothes make the musician," but I can elaborate further upon typical behavior patterns.

The Center. In classical music from 1720 to 1920 or a bit later (already labeled as the "central classical" repertory, performed by tuxedo-clad males and by women in modestly formal evening dress), musicians, when not playing, interact not at all or in accordance with prescribed formal ritual.[11] For example, upon entering the stage, the conductor (ordinarily dressed in some distinct way to that show he or she is in a different class) shakes hands with the concertmaster and asks the orchestra to rise to acknowledge applause. Interaction with the audience is similarly formal. Performers do not speak to the audience except perhaps to announce encores, and even this is may be done with some visible embarrassment. Otherwise, the interaction is carried out through applause and bows, at most going as far as calls of "bravo!" and presentation of flowers on stage. The audience's dress is relatively formal; one sees many men in suits and few without neckties. There is a degree of correlation between formality of audience dress, cost of tickets, and size of the production. Thus, the most formal dress is found in opera audiences, followed by symphony orchestra, chamber music, and, finally, solo piano recitals.

New Music. The ensemble of a new music concert, most of the time clearly distinguished by its experimental style, tries not to appear in perfect uniform and so dresses informally, often in slacks and turtlenecks and either with or without jackets. The relationship between musicians and audience is usually as formal as in the central classical music performances, although some of the pieces admit or even require informality and closeness, or even audience participation. In contrast to central music, new music scores sometimes include directions to that effect and provide in other ways for nonsonic aspects of the music, such as the soloist's assessment of the piano with a tape measure in John Cage's "Concert for Piano."

Audiences at new music concerts dress informally but not casually; indeed, many individuals dress like the performers, and, although there is much variety, this similarity may reflect the audience's desire to identify with the musicians, expressing solidarity with what is sometimes considered a downtrodden and neglected sector of the musical world. Further, composers, performers, and listeners at new music concerts are, to a greater degree than in the other genres, the same people. Even when this is not the case, the impression of unity of performers and audience in new music concerts is remarkable and comparable to that of ethnic concerts.

Jazz at the U. Although the type of jazz performed in the university does not really correspond to the important types of jazz heard in the real musical world, jazz is regarded as a separate category. In the music school one rarely hears solo or small ensemble performances; normally, it is "big-band" jazz. The ambivalence about the place of jazz within the music taxonomy is reflected in a certain ambivalence of dress codes. Musicians may dress uniformly, although normally they wear something like nonmatching trousers and sports jackets or blazers. But sometimes they appear in tuxedos or formal suits. In general, the performances are formal, and the musicians' dress and behavior share the characteristics of their tuxedo-clad colleagues. However, the leader or conductor addresses the audience, announcing pieces (there is no printed program), giving some background about individual musicians and works, telling about recent and forthcoming tours of the group, and possibly even making some jokes. After a number, the leader calls out the names of soloists, who rise or walk forward to take bows. During a piece, soloists may move from their seats and walk to the front of the ensemble, facing the audience while playing. The audience dresses informally, and more children attend jazz concerts than central or new music events. Many men who wear sweaters may have been seen wearing suits at the previous night's symphony concert.

Ethnic Events. There is a category for which I will use the term *ethnic* concerts, some of them performed by members of the school and others by people brought in for education and entertainment. Included here are events such as folk song concerts, performances by a resident Russian folk orchestra populated by Americans, a chorus of African Americans (and a few others) labeled the "Black Chorus," and a visiting chorus of gospel singers. What is unique about ethnic concerts is a real, or at least presumed, identification of the performers and their music with the audience, not only in musical, but also in social and cultural, senses. The basic assumption is that an ethnic concert is directed to a particular audience comprised of members of an ethnic or racial group or of a social or political movement, at least so it is perceived by many participants and by outsiders, for whom this association becomes the main cause of their abstinence.

Typically, the performers' dress is in some way symbolic of the ethnic group in question. Traditional rural folk costumes are common, but contemporary dress, brightly colored choir robes, or uniformly plaid shirts may also be worn. The leader of the group usually addresses the audience before the performance and between the numbers, using a tone that assumes performers and audience to be an exclusive group and the event a conspiracy against the establishment. Not usually explanatory of the music, the remarks introduce individuals, delve (usually by implication) into their personal lives and attitudes, perhaps include anecdotes, and may be mildly deprecatory—with a wink—of the music being performed. There are expressions and "in" jokes thought to be intelligible only to the ethnic audience. All together, in contrast to the central classical concert that maintains distance between performers and audience, the people attending an ethnic concert seem to feel themselves more of a homogeneous group. The informal dress of the audience is characteristic— blue jeans, leather jackets, and no neckties, or sometimes, by contrast, conspicuous, formal dress.

The Exotic Corner. The concerts of non-Western music, particularly by student groups such as a gamelan, by local faculty such as a sitar teacher, or by visiting groups such as a Japanese classical ensemble, share characteristics with both ethnic and classical concerts.[12] The audiences include many members of the nationality whose music is being performed, and to them it is actually an ethnic event. For the other members of the audience, such concerts are often educational rather than esthetic experiences.

An (Asian) Indian concert at Heartland U. is seen as a way of drawing the local Indian community together and fostering respect for Indian culture; dress thus is very formal, and members of the audience interact enthusiastically before the concert and during the intermission. American members of the audience, faculty and students, exhibit no consistency in dress. The performers wear traditional Indian costume, whether they are in fact Indians or Americans and no matter what they may wear every day.

The interaction with the audience is a mixture of traditional and educational. Thus, someone introduces the Indian performers—a distinguished non-Indian faculty member or administrator may be considered as ideal for this role—giving, in a style sometimes used in India, the musical genealogy of performers but often also providing some factual material about the music, as one might do it in a classroom. Communication between performers and audience is much like that of Western classical concerts, except that the performers may feel called upon to explain their music and the instruments. Increasingly, the explanation is contained in printed program notes, and yet one of the performers frequently addresses the audience at some point, drawing this type of event part-way toward the style of presentation of an ethnic concert.

Early Music. Early music—medieval, Renaissance, and early Baroque—is performed at special concerts by ensembles generally called "collegia musica." This body of music is kept quite separate from the central classical repertory. Special instruments (although this early repertory could also be played on standard instruments), special costumes often based on dress in Elizabethan England, and attempts to make these events partially into educational events associate early music concerts with those of non-Western music. The two types also share patterns in audience behavior and the relationship between performers and audience.

A type of musical event that was widespread in colleges and universities as well as high schools during the 1960s and 1970s, and was still provided occasionally during the 1980s, is the madrigal dinner. Taking place before Christmas, it is simply a formal dinner (for which one purchases tickets) after which a choral group, dressed in Elizabethan costume, renders sixteenth- and early seventeenth-century vocal music, largely secular and prevailingly from the repertory of the so-called English madrigal school of around 1580–1640. Sometimes the singers also serve the dinner. Usually there is little religious Christmas spirit, but somehow the concept of early music has become attached to that of Christmas and to a festive and definitely red-meat-oriented meal.

The Untouchables. The kinds of music performances described so far account for the majority of concerts in the Music Building, but

musical life in the surrounding university and local community includes also other kinds of music and social contexts. Primarily, they
are rock and related genres and country and western music performed
in bars or nightclubs. Here, too, musicians wear traditional although
not predictable costumes. The main thing about rock groups is that
no two members of a group dress identically, and some costumes may
be described as highly outré. Country music performers may wear
ordinary farm or work clothes, or sometimes spectacular outfits related to these; in any event, they wear no dress suits, tuxedos, spiffy
uniforms, or torn T-shirts, but rather outfits that somehow symbolize the middle of the middle class, the group described in newspa-
pers during the 1970s as "middle America."

In the Music Building, however, rock and country music groups
appear "once in a blue moon."[13] When they do, they can be readily
associated in terms of the musicians' behavior and audience-performer
relationship with some of the musics mentioned earlier—the new
music concerts in the case of rock, ethnic concerts in the case of
country and western. But the occasion arises rarely. More typically,
music school teachers prefer that their students avoid contact with
these musics lest they become irrevocably polluted. The similarity of
the concentric circle structure (in which musics in the Music Building relate to each other) to a colonial system is suggestive. Musics
outside the central repertory may enter the hallowed space by way
of a servants' entrance: classes in musicology. They may be accepted
(performed) as long as they behave like the central repertory (performed in concerts with traditional structure) but remain separate (no
sitar or electronic music in an orchestral and quartet concert). It is
difficult to avoid a comparison with the colonialist who expects the
colonized native to behave like himself (take up Christianity and give
up having two wives) but at the same time to keep his distance (avoid
intermarrying with the colonialist population).[14]

Bringing the Past to the Present

The Musics of History
Each Society Has Its Own Music History. We have considered a view
of the world as a group of separate musics, a view modeled in part
on the Western conception of society more pronounced in the past

than in the late twentieth century. In this view, the combination or mixing of ethnic or culture groups must be managed with care to avoid pollution. The conception of world music as *musics* is, however, also based on the Western perception of art music as a repertory whose components are principally distinguished by their times of origin. Much of the energy of the music school is devoted in various ways to bringing the past to the present.

Nowhere is history simply "what happened"; it is always interpreted in ways that are determined by, and support, fundamental values and principles of culture.[15] Even where societies have little concrete information about their own musical past, they still have ideas and beliefs of what happened based on myth, folklore, and oral tradition; they also have some ideas of how music history "works," about its mechanisms of change and continuity.[16] At the same time, these societies, which have factual information through detailed written records, may nevertheless ignore them in favor of interpretations of history based on mythical, social, or political values. Each society has its own history in at least two senses because each music history is in part the invention of music historians.[17]

Learning something of the way in which a society interprets its history—whether or not a lot of hard data is available—is central to the ethnomusicological purpose. For example, although they hardly enunciated a specific theory on the subject, Blackfoot people in the 1960s and 1970s appeared to view their music history as principally comprised of three periods that correlate with different ways of composing music: (1) a prehistoric period in which the world was peopled in part by mythic characters who brought the earliest songs into the world; (2) Blackfoot culture before the coming of whites, when music came about mainly through dreams in which supernatural beings taught songs to humans; and (3) the time since the onset of Westernization, when Indian songs were mostly composed consciously by individuals. The Blackfoot also talked about past events in music, largely in terms of the introduction of different genres, ceremonies, or dances to their nation. Their periodization involved considerations of musical style and compositional methods, but not the lives of individual singers, composers, or songs.[18]

As a second illustration, around 1970, I studied with musicians in the Iranian classical tradition who had available a certain amount of literature on the history of music by Iranian scholars, but this did not seem to affect their fundamental approach to the history of their music. They seemed to divide the topic into two major periods, the second beginning with the work of musicians who, about 1880, established the classical system in its contemporary form. To the musicians, those 110 years were full of many events; they viewed the time before that as compressed, and the pre-Islamic era, when it is thought that much of musical value was accomplished, seemed not so long ago, providing a telescoped view. The things to which Iranian musicians seem to tie their historical consciousness are individual musicians of the past and the existence of modal units, called *maqams,* *dastgahs,* and *gushehs.* They were concerned to determine which (or which of their names) were old, when they entered the repertory, and where they came from. It was important to the musicians to determine that something was old. And, in general, they emphasized the stability of the musical system, trying to show that things had not really changed very much rather than the opposite.

Musicians in the Carnatic tradition have documentary material available to them, much more than is the case for Iran. But what, among the many available facts and events, seems most significant to them? In my limited experience with them, Carnatic musicians were concerned with the distant past and with origins, and they seemed to see their history as populated by outstanding individuals who invented things, provided innovations. Yet they did not state the facts in terms of a musical system that undergoes change, but of separable events that signal the origins of new practices. Although they admitted that change occurs, and that much change has occurred as the result of Westernization of musical thought and culture, they stressed the significance of continuity and the undesirable qualities of innovation.

In many cultures, it seems to be important to people to emphasize that their music is ancient; that it is in some sense a pure expression of the culture; that it is distinct from the music of other societies; and, in many cases, that it is of superior quality, or at least that it exceeds Western music in some specific respects. Possibly nowhere is this specialness of a culture's music stressed more than among musicians and their audiences in Europe and, within that context, perhaps nowhere more than in the world of European classical or art music.

Periods and Eras. Music Building society typically reacts to a piece of music initially by identifying its period of composition. Music students learn about periods of music history very early in their courses of study. The periodization of music history is one of the abiding issues of musicology, and several schemes of periods have been promulgated, but the six-period plan (Medieval, Renaissance, Baroque, Classical, Romantic, and Twentieth Century) is most widely accepted in American courses and textbooks.[19]

Although any teaching of history would necessitate subdivision of a continuum, the approach of American music history teachers is worthy of comment. It is an approach very much concerned with boundaries and sees the periods as separable musics in the way that ethnomusicologists see the world of music as consisting of discrete musics. As evidence I cite not only the usual arrangement of texts and courses, but also the requirements of performance majors in their recitals; for example, one might be required to present music from, say, the Classical, Romantic, and Contemporary periods. And just as ethnomusicologists have usually tried to provide a picture of "a" music by sketching its most stable and consistent characteristics, music historians have been typically concerned with the centers of periods by asking, for instance, what makes Baroque music what it is, or what is the most typical sort of Romanticism, or whether the Renaissance centers on Josquin or Palestrina. They have usually not been quite as concerned with the transitions—the Mannheim school, Weber, Debussy, Satie, Ives. There is, at least in the teaching of music history in music schools, more emphasis on stability than on change and on the consistency of directions once they are established. When quizzed with recordings, American students seem better able to identify the styles of Mozart, J. S. Bach, and Brahms than works of C. P. E. Bach, late Beethoven quartets, early Stravinsky, or Gesualdo, and they are inclined to look at music history as a complex of motion around a mainstream centered on Bach, Beethoven, and Brahms. If the music school is important as a place in which musics of various societies may meet, then it is also a place of meeting for the musics that comprise the periods of Western music history, providing a place for each but finding ways to keep them separate.

Reactionaries and Radicals. The culture of the Music Building is heavily concerned with questions and issues that are, in the broad sense, historical. Some readers may regard this kind of concern as a specialty of Western high culture, but other societies are probably no different, and although they usually lack a quantity of hard data, they often worry about such things as whether a piece or a genre is old, can be associated with a musical culture hero, or is properly a part of the culture at all.[20] But the special task of the Heartland Music Building appears to be, one might almost say, connecting the present with the past, or with particular points in the past.

The pantheon of great composers consists entirely of men who died about a hundred years ago, or more. The majority of musical works that are performed or studied were composed before their performers were born. In general, what is most emphasized about musical works and styles, about composers and performers, even about instruments, is—broadly speaking—their origin, their place in history. Composers, whose role it is to oppose domination by older music, are concerned with "making history," striving to make changes in musical style, to "be original." Performers of older music are greatly concerned with following the precepts of earlier, authentic, and "original" performance practice. Undergraduates in music take a substantial number of courses in music history, more, for example, than their counterparts in visual art, and graduate students in all fields of music must pass muster in music history to be admitted and graduate. There would seem to be an enormous interest in history, origins, and change; one hardly deals with any subject without bringing up the question of how it came to be and what it has been.

One could, therefore, expect the concept of "music history" to be well loved on the various floors of the Music Building, with music historians esteemed and popular. To be sure, they are hardly the pariahs they sometimes see themselves to be, but most students and teachers are ambivalent about musicologists, sometimes seeing them as a "requirement police." When it comes to the view of history and change, many music students and faculty perceive musicologists as belonging to the conservative or even reactionary part of the musico-political spectrum, emphasizing not only the central classical music but also promulgating the earlier music (note that the early music ensemble, the collegium musicum, is usually under the aegis of musicologists) and insisting on historically accurate performance practice. In my experience, musicologists do (with significant exceptions) take a conservative view of Music Building society, exhibiting attitudes shared by the conservative sector of society at large and criticizing style and content of program notes, misspellings on posters, grammar in the rhetoric of memos, frivolity of graphics, curricular change, and compositional experimentation.

The nature of musicology, its appropriate subject matter, and its relationship to the rest of the musical academy have been widely discussed.[21] Many musicologists look at their contemporary culture as they see (or at least would like their undergraduate students to see) music history, a time line in which stability is more prominent and more desirable than change. Even so, "counting house" at concerts of new music ordinarily shows a relatively strong representation of members of musicology faculties.

In the music school, composers are the principal promulgators of change and see change and innovation as the main characteristics of history and the present. They can be classified in categories from reactionary to radical, but all composers regard innovation in musical style and content as the main requisite of a successful compositional career, if not a successful composition. This attitude characterizes the world of art music composition at large but is more pronounced in the Music Building, where the concept of new music is kept separate from the rest of music. Generally, composers do not attend concerts of central classical music frequently, but are more likely to appear when other musics are performed—early, non-Western, or jazz. Some maintain that knowledge of earlier art music is of no special use to contemporary composers.

The Specialness of Western Music History

The music school is an institution for both study and advocacy—advocacy of the Western art music tradition, particularly in the common-practice period, 1720 to 1920. We should not be surprised that its view of the history of Western music and, indeed, of world music derives from this purpose. Judith Becker suggests that Western musicians regard their music as superior in three respects: (1) it is based on natural principles, and forces of nature moved it through stages that are now represented by other musics of the world to its present form or, more properly, to its form in nineteenth-century Europe, its highest state of achievement; (2) it is more complex than other musics and in a totally different class of complexity; and (3) it has meaning in a way that other musics do not.[22] "Western music is just too different" [from all the rest of the world's music] may be the best-known sentence of Joseph Kerman's book about musicology.[23] Music appreciation teachers sometimes distinguish between Western and other musics by asserting that the Western is dynamic and the rest of the musical world is static.

Other societies also insist on the uniqueness of their own music, but they usually do not suggest that it ought to be adopted by all other cultures. Western musicians, like the Western politicians of yore, impose their music on the rest of the world. Western society regards its culture as different from the rest, not only in degree but also in kind and reflects this in its attitude toward music. Westerners distinguish their music by insisting that it has a distinct history, a history in which the other musics of the world play supporting roles.

World Music and Music History. What is the role of non-Western music in the Music Building's conception of music history? The typical music history course regards world music history, as Becker suggests, as a single event. On the basis of textbooks and styles of teaching we can identify two approaches to explanation:

There is a linear scheme in which Western music is divided into six periods, all of essentially equal value, preceded by a stage that encompasses ancient, oriental, tribal, and perhaps also European folk musics. In considering the musics of the world, and those no longer extant, older textbooks and some music history teachers take a view that is primarily historical. They consider the differences among the world's musics as historical phenomenon, with all cultures moving through similar stages at different speeds. Non-Western musics have not yet attained, or barely begun, to reach the stage of European medieval music and have thus been presented very briefly preceding consideration of Pythagoras, Plato, and Aristoxenos. But the periods of Western music, as seen in Grout's popular text or in the Prentice-Hall Music History series, are roughly equal in amount and detail of coverage.[24]

A second approach gives the same role to non-Western music but extends it somewhat to earlier and the most recent Western art music. Music rises from tribal and oriental to early Western music and finds its apex in the period of Bach, Mozart, and Beethoven, after which there is again a decline. The period from 1730 to 1830 receives the most attention and the most space, and what happened after Beethoven is seen, in the long run, as response to Beethoven's challenge.

The idea of directionality is made clear in arrangements and titles and subtitles. Early music is important simply because it is old and because it led to the great achievements of the eighteenth and nineteenth centuries; the twentieth century and other kinds of music receive less attention. Typical music history or music appreciation textbooks still exhibit this view, although perhaps not as strongly as previously. In the large and very successful textbook by Stolba, the twentieth century occupies about 15 percent of the total space, although vast amounts of data are available for the period, in which there is participation (in the Western art music enterprise) on the part of musicians from more European and American cultures than ever and for which the total population of musicians, audiences, media, and styles might well suggest a much greater proportion of coverage. The same order of proportion (16 percent) is available for the twentieth century in Stanley Sadie's music appreciation text, *Music Guide*.

The early music period, up to 1600, whose music is far less known (or appreciated) than that of later eras, occupies 33 percent of Stolba's book, which is explicitly an accounting of history; it comprises as much as 12 percent of Sadie's book, a work whose purpose is to provide a guide to listeners, with historical orientation less strongly emphasized. The emphasis in both books on the eighteenth and nineteenth centuries reflects music school life and the placement of names in Harvard's Paine Hall, but the distribution of other musics within the musicological universe clearly favors the early, attends to the conservative aspects of the twentieth century, and avoids or segregates the popular into other chapters.

In other texts, twentieth-century art music has begun to occupy substantial proportions of space, and noncanonic Western music and the music of other cultures have gradually come in for slightly more extensive and generally more dignified treatment.[25] Many of the most influential music historians saw a central strand of history leading from Bach to Beethoven, to Brahms and Bruckner, perhaps Wagner and even Schoenberg, with everything else clustering about this strand at various distances.[26] The concentric circle principle is at work, as the periphery began in Spain, England, Scandinavia, and Hungary and moved out to rural genres and other continents

Reconciling Opposites. An important aspect of the Music Building's view of its own music involves the need to reconcile opposites: the value of the old and of change, opposite poles, and that of origins.

The contrastive values of the old and of change are paradigmatic in Western society's view of art music. It is a view that has been around for a long time. In the world of European art music, it seems likely that historical consciousness did not play a major role until the Renaissance, with its desire to return to ancient classical ideals. But before that, in the distinction made between *ars antiqua* and *ars nova* in the early fourteenth century and the insistence that something new was afoot about 1600 suggest that the contrast between new and old—and a dynamic view of history—played a major role.

By the eighteenth and nineteenth centuries, the concept of progress and the desire of composers to stay ahead of their audiences and competition had become established. At that point, music, to be alive, must always be (or claim to be) changing. But the possibility of holding onto the old while forging ahead increased as methods of transmission became more fixed—first through the exclusively aural and through handwritten notation that had little standardization, then on to higher degrees of agreement and printing, and eventually to recording and synthesis.

In the twentieth century, a major motivating force has been the desire to see music expand. There is a resulting paradox. On the one hand is the belief that composers must constantly do things that are new, not only in essence but also in kind. Pieces must not only be new in their specific content (themes, sequences of harmonies, or tone series), but they must also show the composer as an innovator in compositional conception, method, and technique. Each work must be a new piece in an established style of composition; the style should be in some sense new. Well, this is one view of history as contemporary composers of new music composers conceive of it. On the other hand, the art music-loving populace, and even some ever-innovating composers, regard the best music as having been created in the past. Even experimentalists of the 1980s have asserted to me that the greatest composers lived a century or two ago, and the most recent of these have only come into the circle of the most respected long after their deaths. After all, Wagner and Brahms, now among the greats, were viewed askance by a large segment of American music lovers into the 1930s; Mahler, into the 1950s. The world of art music has a bifurcated view of the value of history and change: It is essential to innovate, but since the time of Mozart and Beethoven (or, in the case of a few radicals, of Wagner or even Schoenberg) music has not been improved.

In elementary school or in the first month of piano lessons, students learn the first great dyad of Western music, major and minor, as tonality, chord, and interval. The tendency to think dualistically continues to play a major role in the perception of music, and so aspects of history are seen in terms of contrasts, dichotomies, and pairs. The most influential forms—sonata-allegro, three-part song form, and rondo—all specialize in presenting contrasts and oppositions; the concerto, growing out of antiphony. The tendency is to present the world of music as pairs of contrastive units (and of pairs of composers for memorization): sacred-secular, vocal-instrumental, program music-absolute music (Wagner-Brahms), supernatural-human (Mozart-Beethoven), local-universal (Bach-Handel), and Schoenberg and Stravinsky (sternly breaking with the past versus growing away from it by stages). Such characterizations are usually historically incorrect or at least oversimplified. That they—and the other dyads—are widely accepted in twentieth-century thought suggests that the world of art music thinks of its field as importantly dualistic. The music school's view of music history is informed by this tendency to dualism.

Ancestry is of great import to the culture of the Music Building, but the performer's interest in history, contrary to the historian's, focuses mainly on its "origins" aspect. The Western conception of art music is closely associated with the concept of history, but history in a special sense. Of course, the most important aspect of a piece of music is its origin, but the origin of pieces includes the questions of how they came about: what their composers had in mind, their identities, how they worked and brought materials together, their stylistic and thematic sources, and the particular form the pieces had at their origins. This emphasis on origin resulted in the concern for authenticity of performance practice, but history in other senses may be ignored by musicians. The social and cultural context of the piece at its moment of origin and its history further on, the so-called reception history, ordinarily interest only scholarly specialists.

Confrontation: Convergences and Collisions

Confrontation of musics has always been the basic stuff of music history and musical culture, much as cultural confrontation is a major characteristic of human behavior. There are many ways in which musical institutions deal with such confrontations, with the issues that arise from their having become meeting places of musics. Intermusical contact plays a role in many of the decisions that result from its concepts and values, decisions that result in behavior patterns and policies which, in turn, lead to characteristics of musical sound at many levels.

Because the Music Building is a locus in which musics from many places, segments of society, and historical origins meet and confront each other, their confrontation is evident in various situations, venues, and events. They meet in the lives of individuals, in the combination of styles by composers and performers, and in institutions such as classes and libraries. Some confrontations result in convergence, but others produce collisions and separation. Although the Music Building absorbs all of these kinds of music and thus provides a venue for musical cultures to meet, this must be done by conforming to standards developed in the world of the central classical repertory and its twentieth-century concert culture. The meeting of musics is encouraged or inhibited in at least three ways: the preservation of the purity of the music, specialized audiences, and ensemble playing.

Preserving Purity

In various ways, the concept of purity, one of the governing values of Heartland music schools, militates against the meeting-place function of the Music Building. To be sure, the "impure," the stylistically and culturally mixed, has its place, but what is in some sense "pure" is often privileged. Thus, concerts remain inside their taxonomic boundaries; you don't find a string quartet performing before the intermission and a sitarist after, or an orchestral work preceded by piano solo (contrary to the substantial variety of program arrangements in Beethoven's time). Except in iconoclastic new music concerts a jazz pianist, a collegium musicum, and a piano trio wouldn't share an evening. In another sense, the value of purity is illustrated in the music school's great interest in authentic performance, on so-called authentic instruments of the composer's time, and in works rendered in accordance with composers' presumed intentions and ideals.

Because the importance given to periods of stylistic stability, central styles, and periods in a composer's career (and the relative neglect of the unclear boundaries between them) is a function of the importance of origins, it seems to be a function as well of the value given to purity. Attention is focused on the static, not on the changing. Along quite another line, students are not strongly encouraged by their primary teachers to perform or hear music outside their major field of interest. Such attitudes inhibit the meeting of musics.

The Heartland music school evidently has a stake in a certain degree of musical coexistence. One might thus expect to see the emergence of performances with combinations of musical style or repertory. Combinations of that kind (sometimes including elements of Western music) are significant in the concert performances by national or nationalistic music and music and dance ensembles in Asian and African nations. Actually, in the music school, the influence flows mainly from the central style to the peripheral ones. East European folk music is accepted when it is performed by large ensembles—the Russian folk orchestra, with its organization analogous to the symphony, and the Balkan choir, analogous to the concert choir. The large jazz band, a miniature of the concert band, plays from scores a substantial amount of music that may lack improvisation. This kind of big-band jazz has a very modest role in the outside world of jazz, but the school nevertheless selects it to be the exemplar of jazz within its walls.

The Specialized Audience

In the kind of town where Heartland U. is located, the music school and its associated performance institutions have a large potential audience—a community of fifty to a hundred thousand. Although a precise count is not available, concert-goers of some regularity are far fewer. In highly approximate estimate, there may be some three hundred music students who attend concerts regularly (out of eight hundred music students in residence), eighty music professors, about a hundred students from other departments, and about three hundred nonmusic university employees and townspeople who appear occasionally. Although there is significant overlapping, different concert types tend to have specialized audiences. They are divided along various lines: by ethnicity, level of education, political attitude, and, most obviously, age. If we can describe American society as comprised of a multitude of ethnicities, white American Anglo cultures are importantly divided by age, each group with its typical ethnic music. For example, the audience of central classical concerts is oldest, and that of new music and ethnic events, youngest. Although chamber music and organ concerts attract older audiences than symphony concerts, jazz concerts claim an older audience than the concert band. In the meeting of musical cultures in the Music Building only a small group of people attend performances of all or several of the musics.

The Worthiness of Ensembles

Another look at the requirement that each student perform in an approved ensemble sheds some light on the role of the music school as a polymusical mediating institution. The majority of the forty or so ensembles characteristic of one school work under conductors and perform music from the period from 1700 to 1930. Jazz bands, gamelan, string quartet, mbira and panpipe, and new music ensembles either perform music outside this period or do not clearly have a conductor (although there is leadership by a faculty member). To persuade the administration or the majority of the faculty that these ensembles should be accepted as fulfilling the requirement has always been difficult for students and faculty who are concerned with them (although in the end they have often succeeded), but it has sometimes been made clear that the school's administration would prefer to have students perform in symphony orchestra, band, and large chorus.

Ensembles outside the central classic framework must prove their worth either by performing music that is in some ways similar to the central art music or by at least operating in ways similar to the large ensembles, by using printed music and having a conductor. Thus, the Russian folk orchestra is successful because it plays from scores and parts, has a conductor, and uses functional harmony in arrangements of traditional Russian folk tunes. The gamelan succeeds because its adherents argue that there is actually a conductor (even though that person does not stand in front) and also by pointing out that, among non-Western ensembles, it comes closest to large Western ensembles in its internal structure and that of its music. Certain Middle Eastern, Latin American, and African ensembles are included because they require few members and may incidentally satisfy certain political needs of the institution. Rock groups and certain other popular ensembles meet none of the criteria and may thus remain in the "untouchable" category.

When asked to discuss these preferences, music school denizens took for granted the esthetic superiority of the central repertory, particularly of the works for large ensembles. (Conceivably, composers set out to write their best works for these ensembles.) The way in which the music school permits musics to meet but also to keep their "proper" relationships is by privileging the large ensembles and accepting grudgingly, if at all, those of other musics—new, old, jazz, popular, ethnic, and non-Western—and then only to the degree that the other musics adopt the values of the central music. This process is also to be observed in Asian and African nations that have developed orchestras of traditional music and instruments for just this competitive function.

Melting Pot or Mosaic?

Never mind policies, requirements, and values. Musical life in the Heartland music school could be described as a melting pot in which a single flavor dominates, or as a mosaic in which many colors coexist, not on equal terms but each assured of survival.[27] Which interpretation casts better light? It is a question that could equally be asked of the entire world of music in our century.

The influence of non-Western, folk, and earlier music on the central classical repertory and its composers since the Renaissance (but mainly in the last 150 years) is often mentioned in music history courses, but not much is made of it in the music school's world of performance. Rarely, for example, in the structuring of concert or recital programs is thought given to arranging works so as to emphasize this influence, with the use, for instance, of strange vocal styles or costumes (if one can imagine that). More realistically, we do not get to hear programs with groups of works that exhibit a specific influence upon their sound (e.g., a concert of Hungarian folk or folk-derived music as rendered in works by Bartók, Liszt, Brahms, Haydn, and Schubert). In the central classical concert, the meeting of musics is blunted. Thus, a folk tune as a theme in a symphony is harmonized and performed by the traditional woodwinds. An African drum is integrated into the standard percussion section.

Even in concerts outside the framework of the central classical repertory, the sounds of musical cultures meet by approximating classical ideals. The concept of concert itself is not compatible with the traditional performance contexts of much or most non-Western music, nor, for that matter, with authentic contexts of medieval, jazz, and folk performance. The traditional three-hour concert of Madras (already in part a product of Westernization) and the three sets of jazz at a club become, in the music school, ninety-minute concerts with intermissions. There is no thought of replicating a jazz club or holding an African ceremony in the gym. The various musics meet by being placed in a common concert format, having some overlapping of audience, and being subjected to the system of values governing the culture of classical Western music. But in terms of musical style, they do not really meet.

If we view the present macrocosm of world music as a confrontation of musical systems resulting in convergences and collisions, this meeting of musics has had many kinds of results: the total abandonment of certain genres, styles, repertories, and even entire musical systems; the development of syncretic styles and repertories; the increased diversity of musical opportunity for certain individuals; the artificial and compartmentalized preservation of older traditions; and the transfer of discrete traits of music, pluralistic coexistence of music, embracing or rejection of the new. In any one meeting of cultures, a variety of musical results may ensue, but occasionally one predominates.[28] The Heartland music school, which sometimes lays claim to microcosmic reflection, shares in some of these processes but scarcely in others. Individuals are given increased opportunity to become polymusical and, at the same time, artificial preservation of musics—early and non-Western musics in particular—sometimes occurs. Yet repertories are not lost or abandoned, and syncretic styles do not often result.

In the interrelationship of its musics, the Music Building parallels only imperfectly the twentieth-century world of musics. But in its juxtaposition of the central classical repertory to satellite styles deemed less significant, it reflects the modern world more explicitly in the sociocultural sense—the relationship of a dominant culture to its satellites or of a major power to third-world colonies. The traditional culture of the dependent societies had to conform to the values of the central power and yet maintain its distance, adopting Christianity, for example, but eschewing industrialization, or switching to a Western family life-style but avoiding intermarriage. The minority or peripheral musics in the music school tend to maintain separation from the central repertory; jazz and Indian music and even new music do not enter the framework of its concerts or curricula. Yet they must adopt, to exist at all, the social and performance contexts of the central music.

The Heartland music school is a place of musical mediation only to a degree, and it is a venue of both convergences and collisions. Convergence in that individuals are free to participate at least as listeners, or as passive students in courses, in a number of the musics that inhabit the building, and there is a modest degree of stylistic overlap and fusion. But collision in that the musics, as it were, repel each other, maintaining distance and coexisting in the hierarchical social structure that Western academics have long taken for granted, permitted to maintain a modest spot in the institution if they bow to the values of the center. All together, perhaps more mosaic than melting pot.

≈ 4 ≈

Forays into the Repertory

The Shape of a Music

Each society has a musical repertory, but societies differ greatly in the way this repertory is distributed among its members and, more important, in the way they conceive of the repertory and how they see its structure in relationship to the domains of culture to which the music is related. But in each culture, the world of music has, and is perceived to have, shape. For example, the Blackfoot people, or at least some of them, seem to regard their music as a reflection of the cultural system.[1] Each of their rituals, each subdivision of their society, has, at least theoretically, appropriate songs. I was told that the right way to do something was to sing the right song with it, and songs are normally identified by the activities or cultural domains with which they are associated.

Some its musicians see the Persian system of classical music as a reflection of the spectrum of moods and affects because each *dastgah* (mode) has a particular character. It is also a reflection of the numerical organization of culture. There are twelve *dastgahs,* seven of which are principal; many shorter units are organized in groups of three. The number *twelve* applies to other domains, and just as there are twelve imams in Shi'ite Islam and twelve constellations in the zodiac, the twelve musical modes (extant more in theory than practice) cover the entire world. The numbers *three* and *seven* play major roles as well. In both cases, the conception of the musical repertory is, in important respects, congruent with the entire culture. In the classical music of South India, the system of ragas is seen as a hierarchy of sorts, reminiscent of the castes; in North India, it is seen as a reflection of family structure, with the figures of father, mother, and child reflecting kinds and degrees of dependency an relationship.

What is the conception of the musical repertory in the American art music world? As point of departure, take the taxonomies of genres, composers, or degrees of classicalness. Denizens of the Music Building conceive of their musical repertory in several ways: (1) as the belief that there is a central core of the repertory, the most important music; (2) as the suggestion that the Music Building looks at its musical works and their relationship much as it looks at society and the relationship of groups and individuals; and (3) as perception of the role that music plays in performances in which the principal values of the culture are exhibited.

The Principal Works

Even in small societies such as the roughly 150 Suyá, a tribal group of Amazonian Brazil studied by Anthony Seeger, each person knows his or her culture from a particular personal view, and there is not always much congruence among the musical experiences of the individuals.[2] Yet ethnomusicologists usually wish to show that a culture has musical coherence and may thus be inclined to ask, "Is there a *central* repertory, which the society identifies most as its own, or regards as its greatest musical product, or knows best?"

My Blackfoot consultants replied to this kind of question in two ways. Their "most important songs" are the songs of the medicine bundle ceremonies, songs now hardly known and always, as in earlier times, known to only a few people; or, they are the intertribal songs sung at powwows and recognized by most of the people who hear them. In the Carnatic music culture of Madras, I was told that the most clearly central repertory was comprised of songs by the three great composers of the early nineteenth century; those were also the songs most widely performed in the concert repertory. In Iran, my teacher told me that the central music would have been music cast in the *dastgah* of Shur because its character reflects most closely the character of Iranian culture.[3]

Each of these societies seemed to accept the idea that a repertory has a central sector, but each had its own criteria for identifying and characterizing it. For the culture of the Music Building, one obvious approach leads to the work of the great masters. They are one key to this concept. But an ethnomusicological visitor from a distant planet might likely notice first that there are some songs that everybody seems to know and can sing, a group that she may not find attractive but seems to hear a lot. I will begin with this alternative body of music.

Obligatory Songs

According to the Menominee consultants of the ethnographer J. D. Slotkin, in the 1940s the Peyote religion ceremonies of the Menominee Indians had two kinds of songs.[4] Four particular ones had to be sung at four specific moments in the ceremony. The rest—perhaps dozens sung in any one night—were selected by the singers, each in turn singing four songs. Although each singer selected what to sing ("just what come to him"), the songs must be "Peyote songs," either coming from the stock of Peyote songs known to the community or in the appropriate and distinctive Peyote musical style, newly composed or learned by the singer of the moment.

This kind of distinction is characteristic of rituals in many cultures. Certain songs or pieces must be performed each time a ritual is enacted, but others are either specific to the occasion or selected at will by the participants. Students in the Music Building are initiated into this structure early in their music history courses as they learn that the Catholic Mass is divided into the Ordinary, comprised of texts that include the "Kyrie Eleison," "Credo," "Sanctus," and "Agnus Dei" (or their vernacular versions); texts that are recited or sung in each Mass (although not always with the same music); and the Proper, including such sections as the "Gradual," "Alleluia," and "Offertory," with texts specific to the celebration of the particular day. A number of rituals in contemporary religious life, including the services of most Protestant churches, have structures derived from the form of the Mass, and others follow similar principles.[5] Secular rituals follow similar lines. Thus, in a formal American dinner, there is a parallel between apéritifs, appetizers, salad courses, wines, and coffee (which are expected to be present no matter what the content of the soup, main, and dessert courses, and in which there is relatively little variety) and the Ordinarium Missae. The other courses, in which there is much greater variety (any self-respecting hostess will refuse

to serve the same thing to the same guests during a five-year span),
are more like the Proper.[6]

We ask which of the two groups of ritual ingredients is the more
central. In the history of religious art music, although the musical
works that are part of or derived from the Proper of the Mass have
often resulted in more elaborate music, the Ordinary may be regarded
as the heart of the Mass because its components are always there,
always basically alike. The Presbyterian service is made what it is by
the presence of invocation, benediction, Lord's prayer, and recitation
of the Creed, no matter how brilliant and extended the sermon.
However grand the main course, and no matter how exotic the dessert, it's the apéritif, wine, and coffee, in that order, that persuade you
that you are at a formal dinner. The question is, Are rituals in the
Heartland university town (including the music school) shared by virtually the entire society? Are they somehow akin to the concept of
"Ordinarium Missae" of life as a whole, and do they also have a
musical repertory that is always present and could thus qualify as the
community's central musical repertory?

There are quite a few shared rituals. Some are rites of passage:
weddings, graduation ceremonies, birthday parties, retirement celebrations, and, in a sense, funerals. Others involve the year's cycle:
Christmas celebrations, New Year's parties, Thanksgiving dinners, Halloween parties, and Easter celebrations. Still others are seasonal but
less specific; for example, certain sports events and associated rites such
as Homecoming.

I do not include some of the important rituals of major subdivisions of society, but try to look informally at those that may be part
of the experience of all strata and subdivisions. Not included, therefore, are the services of specific churches and other religious congre-
gations, for the community uses such differences to subdivide itself
socially. They have much in common and, as a group, are part of the
culture, but individually they are not shared to the same degree as
the practices of birthday parties, baseball games, or graduations. Nor
do I include the many academic rituals—class examinations, doctoral
orals, the president's tea for new faculty—that are not open to the
community as a whole.

The structure of the shared rituals varies; the *proper* part greatly
outweighs the *ordinary,* but there are aspects in each that can always
be expected, things that always happen. In a baseball game, there is

always the seventh-inning stretch, and at a birthday party there is always the presentation of a cake followed by the blowing out of candles. Some of the things that always happen are musical, and this is the music everybody knows.

Thus, for the rites of passage, at many weddings one expects to hear the wedding march from *Lohengrin* at the beginning and the quicker one from Mendelssohn's *Midsummer Night's Dream* at the end. At birthday parties, one must sing "Happy Birthday," arguably the single best-known musical work in the nation. At graduations, one may feel unfulfilled unless Elgar's *Pomp and Circumstance* number 1 is performed. That was surely the case in the 1950s and 1960s, before greater musical variety was introduced (along with other departures from ritual orthodoxy in the ceremonial life of the Heartlands, including church services). There seems to be no typical work of music for funerals, and retirements—perhaps in analogy with funerals—also are not handled as consistently. "For He's a Jolly Good Fellow" may be the closest thing to obligatory music for retirees.

Following the year's cycle, excepting now the personal cycles of birthdays and wedding anniversaries, the Heartland culture celebrates a number of periods or days that have religious associations but probably (like St. John's Day, which is also summer solstice) have origins in pre-Christian feasts and now, returning perhaps to their origins, may for many people no longer hold much specifically religious content. The most prominent are Christmas, New Year's, Easter, Halloween, and Thanksgiving.

Not all of these celebrations qualify as rituals, and in their secular versions they have no liturgy and no obligatory music, although almost all would include music—performed on organ, or sung by everyone present, or heard on records and tapes—that involves a specific repertory of some breadth: art and vernacular music.

Yet there is performance whose music is predictable and fulfills the function of an Ordinary, at least in vestige. Christmas in particular is a season accompanied by music not heard or performed at other times, such as Handel's *Messiah*. More important, Christmas carols—especially a particular small group of carols selected from the hundreds available in collections—are all but obligatory at the events included in the season's celebration, including church services and parties, informal Christmas gatherings, parties for family or sponsored by employers, and organized carol singing. Caroling groups, ambu-

latory or seated, voluntary association or Sunday school class, preponderantly use a small number of songs that are part of the culture's
central repertory. The principal ritual of the culture, however, is
Christmas dinner, which, according to household custom, either
precedes or follows the opening of presents and is without specific
music. New Year's celebrations are more ritualistic and always include
a special observance at midnight, perhaps a toast, which is often followed by the singing of "Auld Lang Syne."

Easter has no ritual outside church (unless one could call color-
ing eggs and hiding Easter baskets such) and no music outside the
Christian church that is quite as specific. Halloween and Thanksgiving have much-prescribed rituals—the begging ceremony ("trick or
treat") and the festive meal—but again no obligatory music.

A number of celebrations that follow the year's course are official holidays that the government prescribes, such as the Fourth of
July. Among the ceremonial events accompanying these celebrations
are parades—processions of a quasi-military sort—with accompanying music taken from a selected repertory of marches and patriotic
songs. The most widely used march, and thus a piece that most people know, is John Phillip Sousa's "Stars and Stripes Forever," which
may, therefore, claim a place in our central repertory. Moreover, parades and their surrounding activities always include the performance
of at least one of three or four central patriotic songs: "America,"
"America the Beautiful," and "The Star-Spangled Banner." These are
also part of the central ceremonial musical repertory of the community. Even though their specific place in parade rituals is not specified, at some point during the celebration at least one of the songs is
likely to be played, sung, or made the subject of a march.

The use of patriotic music is also a required component of the
ceremonial in the partially calendric sports events such as football,
baseball, and basketball games, many or most of which begin with
"The Star-Spangled Banner," a practice not found in most other rituals or events such as concerts or film showings, except in wartime.
The national anthem's presence suggests the perception of a homology between athletics and war and between athletic teams and military forces, and possibly the belief that athletics is somehow patriotic and a special symbol of American-ness or the nation. Referring
to a football game as a "fight" at which each team's band plays its
"fight song" ("Indiana, My Indiana" or "We're Loyal to You, Illinois,"

or, further east, "Crash Through That Line of Blue") also illustrates the parallel.[7] Music at university sports events usually includes the institution-specific alma mater and fight song. Yet at some point in most baseball games "Take Me Out to the Ball Game" is either played or sung. At Heartland U., musicians at athletic events are preponderantly students in the school of music.

Could we, from this set of considerations, build a notion of a central repertory, and would it indeed include "Happy Birthday" and "Auld Lang Syne," some marches, a collection of Christmas carols, some patriotic songs, perhaps Elgar's "Pomp and Circumstance," the Mendelssohn and Wagner wedding marches, and, perhaps at one time, "I Love You Truly"? Not hard to make a list. It is not what the denizens of the Music Building regard as their culture's great music, and most of it is not serious music to them. Hardly anyone would consider it "good" music, this music associated with the central rituals. Still, it is the music most known and most predictable.

It may all seem strange, and stranger still when we consider that much of the music in the contemporary concert repertory was composed to fulfill a specific ritual function not involving concerts. Much of it was conceived as church music, or as background music for aristocratic dining and partying, or for the stage; some of it was music for specific events, a particular coronation, a birthday party, a hunting party, a wedding, or a victory celebration. But in the art music world of today, it seems inappropriate to associate what we consider to be the best music with specific ritual or ceremonial functions; it is a way of denigrating the music's stature.

One of the characteristics of twentieth-century concert culture is its tendency to combine works that would not, when first composed, have been found on the same program. And so we prefer to forget that some of Mozart's works, for example, would, by their origins, be totally appropriate for each of the ceremonies of the Heartland U. town of the 1980s. The community surrounding the Music Building would, however, be disinclined to demean a great composer by putting much of his music into a functional role. Music Building denizens usually do not feel that Mozart is being honored when his music is used as background music in a film score, as in *Hopscotch*.[8] The Music Building's own ceremonial world lives quite separately. Its rituals are not carried out, in the last analysis, for the sake of humans and their necessary activities, but in the service of the great masters, whose works stand above the hustle and bustle of human coming and going and exist as art for art's sake.

Masterworks

In the preceding section, I suggested that one kind of central repertory is the music everyone knows, but there are other ways of determining centrality. One might look for the music that society considers as the most "normal." Or the music that everyone does not know but, according to some authority, ought to know. Or what about the greatest of works? Do they not deserve status of centrality? In the conversational rhetoric of the Music Building, "great" refers mainly to the largest works. It is no coincidence that in one of the few books about the concept of musical masterworks the first two works mentioned are Mozart's *Don Giovanni* and Wagner's *Ring of the Nibelung.*[9]

We might identify the great works by looking in standard textbooks of music history and literature and of music appreciation. Or by looking at the list of works covered in "Basic Music Literature" and other introductory courses for music majors, or, for that matter, the works doctoral students are expected to know on their comprehensive or qualifying examinations. Another path is simply to ask members of Music Building society what works they consider to be great. The question of popularity and stature of masterworks ought to be subjected to detailed demographic and statistical analysis, and there is a good deal of literature dealing with the issue.[10]

To identify the concept of a central repertory and its general character, although not its content in detail, consider two small samples of Music Building population. Could they easily identify the greatest works, and do they agree on what they are? In the first instance, I tried the question on a group of thirteen graduate students, most from musicology, without warning, simply asking them to write down two or three of the greatest works (or groups of works) in Western art music. There was little unanimity; twenty-seven works were listed. The dominant composers were Bach, Beethoven, Mahler, and Wagner, but also listed (here in alphabetical order) were Bartók, Luciano Berio, Brahms, Debussy, Josquin des Prez, Mozart, Prokofieff, Puccini, Schubert, Schumann, and Shostakovitch. The most prominent genres were operas and symphonies. Only Beethoven's Seventh, Wagner's *Tristan,* and his *Ring* received two votes each. Respondents grouping works listed Beethoven symphonies, Mahler symphonies, Beethoven's and Shostakovitch's late quartets, Debussy preludes, Schubert lieder, Puccini operas, and Bach violin works.

Had I asked for names of composers rather than works, my guess is that Beethoven and Bach would have been there and also Mozart, Haydn, and Schubert, although probably not Wagner and surely not Mahler. When asked to list works, the respondents thought automatically of the long ones requiring major forces. There is reason to believe that the respondents did not know these masterworks works well or at all, but the idea was to list large, complex works. "Greatness" of music consists of length, complexity, and a composer's ability to do the difficult and control a vast number of musical gestures, events, and interrelationships. Given this athletic approach to composition, many American music lovers think that a great work must be physically large. So do academic musicians: To get a doctorate in composition, a student must produce a "large" work.

Second, in 1989 Melinda Russell asked a group of undergraduates not majoring in music but electing to take a course in the Music Building to identify records they would take to a desert island.[11] The classical composers most mentioned were Beethoven, Mozart, Bach, and Mahler, with the Beatles (representatives of a "classic" era as well) coming in after Beethoven. The works most widely mentioned were Beethoven's Fifth and Ninth and his Violin Concerto, also *Götterdämmerung,* Mozart's *Jupiter* symphony, Strauss's *Don Quixote,* and Dvořák's "New World" Symphony. Again, with little specific agreement, there was emphasis on a few major composers and on large, long works with orchestra and perhaps chorus.

The two quite different groups of students provided different answers to the same kind of question differently phrased. But what they had in common was the evident belief that musical greatness resides in bigness and complexity, and that the center of musical greatness lies between 1750 and 1900. Do the typical musical structures of that time reflect the social structure that the American middle-class desires, or was it what society used to desire, or did musical structure and the relationship of musical and social organization just freeze at some point, as Small has suggested?[12] Perhaps we have in the music the kind of society at whose pinnacle many individuals in American society would like to be, but, knowing better than to impose it on real society, they are content to play with it by making it the centerpiece of their music. It's a bit like loving the British monarchy but not living in it.[13]

A Society of Musics

We have been observing a network of social interrelationships. Musicians in the world of art music relate to each other in ways that parallel the social organization of society—familial, class-derived, by division of labor, and also in ways that reflect their roles in musical structures and ensembles. These, in turn, are derived from models such as governmental, religious, military, and productive organizations that are otherwise used in Western society, and from the kinds of hierarchies on which they are based. I have suggested that musicians and lovers of art music see their world as structured somewhat like that of society. The orchestra is a kind of factory, the pantheon of composers like an extended family, the concert like a ritual of worship, and the educational institution like an industrial corporation. Now, I wish to suggest that the kinds of relationships that are evident in the society of people in the Music Building, and in art music generally, play an important role in determining ways in which they conceive of the musical materials themselves—pieces of music, kinds of compositions, and instruments.

Taken together, the majority of works and genres in the standard repertory, comprised largely of music composed between 1730 and 1920, reflect certain prominent principles of our social structure: the importance of and interrelationships in the nuclear family, the hierarchy of classes and their gradations, and the importance of individuality and individual leadership.

Reflections of Family and Community

Classifications and taxonomies in musical cultures have been given substantial attention in ethnomusicological literature, but they have not frequently been the subject of comparative scrutiny. One area of musical life that lends itself most easily to such comparison is the classification of instruments, a field with which Margaret Kartomi deals on an intercultural basis.[14] The selection of taxonomies she examines suggests that the cultures of the world group their instruments in ways modeled on important aspects of their worldviews. The principal Chinese instrument classification system presents the world of instruments as a reflection of the physical world; instruments are classed in one of eight groups determined by the principal material of construction. Arabic classifications provide a hierarchy of status and acceptability, somewhat along the lines of the social and musical hierarchies used in Islamic cultures.

The Choral Paradigm. In the musical culture of the Heartland, music appreciation texts introduce instruments in groups united by acoustic principles, appearance, and function in orchestras or bands. We think of instruments as belonging to families. Among orchestral instruments, the string (or violin) family is the most obvious example, but woodwinds and brasses are also frequently called "families." Such a family is a group of instruments produced in three or four sizes and melodic ranges. The term *family* is not used for all instrument types, such as viols, tubas, clarinets, but with them, too, the tendency has been to develop groups of instruments, each of which consist of three or even four manifestations of the same principle in different size and range. The model for much of this is the vocal choir in which the familial principle—women and men, each with a low and a high voice, perhaps suggesting parent and child—is paradigmatic. Although young men and women do not necessarily have higher voices than those of middle age, the association of soprano and tenor with youth and alto and basso with age is widespread in musical representations such as operatic roles. Instrumental ensembles in which various members of a "family" play together in large numbers are also often called "choirs," for example, the clarinet choirs and trombone choirs found in the list of ensembles at a Heartland school.

The concept of family as a guiding principle for terminology in the grouping of instruments is found in other cultures as well, for example in the use of family relationships in the classification of African instruments and their parts.[15] In the twentieth century, non-Western societies have often adopted the Western principle of family construction of instruments. Thus, in Iran, the traditional *gheichak,* a bowed string instrument of intermediate range, was expanded to several forms—soprano, tenor, and bass—for use in orchestras. The balalaika and *domra* orchestras of Russia have likewise established soprano, alto, tenor, and bass versions of the instruments and thus consist of two principal sections, each analogous to the art music string orchestra. The same has been true of modern Chinese orchestras, and attempts have been made in the past to create such group-ings in Indian music with the introduction of double-bass sized *sa-rangis* (north Indian bowed instruments). The development of orches-tras from "choirs" of traditional instruments seems to be one of the pervasive patterns of musical westernization.[16]

The four-part principle as the norm virtually dominates the stan-dard repertory of Western art music. In the Music Building, it is there not only in instrumental and vocal combinations—chamber groups, sections in orchestras, even rock groups—but also in theory classes and in the interrelationship of works and genres of music. The mu-sical system is taught with the use of four voices, four-tone chords. Learning how the use of four voices provides underpinnings for the fundamental guidelines composing and understanding music is an important component of musicians' training.

There may be important musical acoustic justifications for the power of the four-part harmony system and the four-part choir and its instrumental analogues. They include the importance of the triad and the need to double its principal tone and also the need for four voices to articulate a seventh chord. But it also makes sense to be-lieve that music reflects important features of society and does not come about in isolation. Regardless of how the four-part system in harmony, choral practice, and instrument families began during the late Renaissance and early Baroque period, it is significant that it has held on tenaciously and continued throughout the twentieth centu-ry to represent the central music. During the nineteenth century, new groups of instruments such as the saxophones, saxhorns, and flugel-horns developed in four-part families, and it is perhaps no coinci-dence that four-part families of instruments gained in ascendancy as harmonic practice increasingly departed from the strict four-part model.

Why do music theory curricula still hang on to four-part struc-ture and the music most associated with it when it plays such a small role in electronic and computer music or, for that matter, in the new music of contemporary composers as a whole? I can suggest a con-tributing factor. As other motivations faded, one may have come to look to the homology of choir with what became widely (in West-ern Europe and North America) regarded as the ideal family—two parents, a son and a daughter—or at least of a family with four dis-tinct roles. To be sure, despite the correlation of age and low pitch, there are ways in which the soprano–alto–tenor–bass structure fails to correspond to the family model. The melody is carried, after all, by the "daughter" voice, superior in its demands and its function to that of the alto "mother" voice. But the four-part structure does reflect some major tensions in family and between genders and generations in society—and this perhaps accounts for its amazing tenacity.

Solo and Accompaniment. If one central component of mainstream Western society is the nuclear family, another is the concept that there is normally a leader or boss in a group, as well as followers or employees. In society, the idea that someone or something is being "accompanied" by something else is constantly present—boss and employees, chair and department, sergeant and military platoon, quarterback and football platoon, pitcher and fielders, president and cabinet, king and roundtable—and, in most, cases father or mother and family, grandfather and extended family as well. Not only is there a hierarchy, but also there is usually one leader and more than one follower.

I have tried to interpret the central repertory as a reflection of the importance of the family concept. Perhaps more important, this repertory also reflects the larger and essentially hierarchical principles of Western social organization. I have already noted the importance of hierarchies in ensembles, but perhaps an even clearer reflection is the centrality of the principle of accompaniment, whose pervasive nature is one of the things that unites the otherwise enormously varied music of the central repertory. Most of it consists of something essential being accompanied by something subordinate. As defined by the list of genres given previously, it consists of piano accompanied by orchestra in the concerto, violin or cello by the piano in solo work and even in extended sections of chamber works such as sonatas, and singing accompanied by the piano or guitar. Indicative of an unyielding social order, the central repertory is music in which the first violin section is accompanied by the rest of the strings, operatic soloists are supported by orchestra, and the strings of the orchestra are supported by the winds. But there is also the pianist's right hand, which is accompanied by the left, and even the hands on the organ are accompanied by feet.

Does music history follow social history? To be sure, as the lower classes of the late 1800s and 1900s were afforded occasional social mobility (or its illusion), the accompanying forces were given opportunities to solo, the left hand occasionally taking the melody, the woodwinds dominating in the trio of the orchestral minuet, and the lieder accompaniments of Schumann featuring piano codas. But the classics, with their structural hierarchy, maintain their centrality in later musical life. The pretense that there is social mobility is maintained, even in its general absence.

A survey of works played on listener-request classical programs at Heartland U. shows that the best-loved pieces exhibit the principle of featured soloistic virtuosity with subservient accompaniment by large forces. Here may lie the reason for the popularity of opera and orchestral music; of concertos; in other respects of virtuosic pieces such as Chopin's polonaises and études or Liszt's piano works; and, in yet other ways perhaps, of "The Flight of the Bumblebee"—even when performed on the tuba.

Some Genres and Forms

The importance of the music from 1720 to 1920 in the contemporary world of art music is in some measure due to the way the musical works reflect aspects of Western middle-class social structure and values in the first half of the twentieth century. The works themselves represent a considerable number of genres. The E. T. ethnomusicologist might well make a list (in random order) of types of works most represented in the core repertory, a list that might be somewhat like the following (also in random order):

Symphonies, followed by shorter orchestral works;
Concertos, mainly for violin or piano with orchestra;
Lieder by nineteenth-century German composers;
Operas by Mozart, Verdi, Wagner, and Puccini, and less by other composers;
Solo piano (and other keyboard) music by Chopin, Beethoven, Mozart, Bach, Schubert, Schumann, and Liszt (this includes short—that is, "character"—pieces, sonatas, suites, and prelude-and-fugue combinations);
Solo violin music, mainly sonatas with piano;
Virtuoso works, usually short, for many instruments but particularly piano and violin, by nineteenth-century non-German composers; and

Chamber music, most often string quartets, with piano trios and piano quintets following.

The Martian would provide evidence of the centrality of this repertory in contemporary art music culture through examination of concert programs, record store holdings, and listener request programs on classical radio stations. The importance of certain genres and functional harmony is reflected in the absence of composers usually regarded as towering figures from other periods.

My purpose is to consider some aspects of this repertory in terms of its internal variegation, texture, and shape in order to ask which works and genres within it occupy central or superior positions, and how they function in their relationship to the whole.

The Ruling Class of Music. This is music for which the term *great* is often used. Conversations among music lovers often move to discussions of relative greatness of composers, performers, works, and performances, and one may hear suggestions that a few works can be singled out as the "greatest." *Don Giovanni* has been listed as the greatest human art work.[17] "C'est l'empereur," cried the French officer upon hearing the Fifth Piano Concerto (so the legend tells us, and we like to believe it although it probably didn't happen). "The 48" is what musicians called "The Well-Tempered Clavier," testifying to its basic character (and maybe also to the numerological significance of the number forty-eight).

These great works, others like them, and the central repertory as a whole exhibit important social values of their period and tensions among them; they also suggest that these same values and tensions are still with us. It is particularly interesting that these greatest works are largely from the eighteenth and first three-quarters of the nineteenth centuries, and that a great deal of what the art music world regards as the world's greatest music was composed before 1825. A vast body of literature tries to explain this greatness as the result of individual genius, of a fortuitous balance between "content and form," as the result of something objectively better than music composed earlier or later.

Ethnomusicologists, accustomed to cultural relativism, are, however, disinclined (for better or worse) to believe that some music may be intrinsically "superior," as might be certain forms of agriculture, industrial production, or medicine.[18] Still, is it not conceivable that certain composers and groups of composers or musical cultures simply discovered better ways of producing music, and that this ability is recognized by later musicians and listeners? What, after all, might account for the relative homogeneity of musics in Sub-Saharan Africa compared to the enormously varying social and cultural systems of the continent, to give one example?

The question has relevance because technique of composer and performer can be judged according to agreed-upon criteria, and we should not regard all individual judgments as equally valid. But these criteria make a difference, and an ethnomusicologist's task is to discover them, society by society, and discover as well their source in individual and group. Looking at the greatest works from the late eighteenth and early nineteenth centuries, and the role they play in contemporary musical culture, we are again tempted to ask whether modern music lovers are most comfortable with music reflecting a social structure that precedes the social upheavals of the French Revolution and the nineteenth and early twentieth centuries.

It is no surprise that these greatest of works are large in various respects and require great forces. The two most representative genres are opera and concerto. It is possible although perhaps not easy to make a case for these two types of music as best representing the principles of late eighteenth-century society. It is easier to show how they represent the kinds of musico-social relationships found in all kinds of eighteenth-century art music—song, sonata, cantata, divertimento, suite, symphony, and all the rest—but represent them to a higher degree, a greater extent. Can they perhaps be interpreted as the ruling class of the society of musics?

Take the operas of Mozart, beginning with the exemplar of all opera, *Don Giovanni,* and see how they illustrate and generalize characteristics of eighteenth-century social structure as perceived by contemporary society. The music exhibits hierarchies of all sorts. The score is an exercise in the complexities of a class system, and the relationship between characters and musical styles often goes along. Serious music is given to the upper classes in the dramatis personae: Donna Elvira, Don Ottavio, Donna Anna, and even the briefly living (and later briefly dead) Commendatore. The misbehaving upper-class figure, Don Giovanni, is a baritone (unconventional for a main character) and sings somewhat humorous music (he really shouldn't belong to the upper classes, his behavior is hardly that of a proper aristocrat). The lower-class characters—the servant, Leporello, and the peasant couple, Zerlina and Masetto—sometimes sing in an arguably folklike or humorous vein. Mozart departs from practices of earlier eighteenth-century opera, where leading men and women inevitably sang the most difficult and spectacular passages, with a clear hierarchy among characters and roles and, as a result, among the performers themselves. Leading characters, who were typically gods, heroes, and kings, were tenors; servants and villains were baritones.

In contrast to the general practice of early and mid-eighteenth-century opera, the late eighteenth-century operas most loved in the twentieth century, those of Mozart, the great masterworks *Don Giovanni* or *The Marriage of Figaro,* and, for that matter, *Così fan tutte* and *The Magic Flute,* go further than simply representing or going along with the inequalities and inequities of society. They also provide a critique of the system. Mozart selected appropriate librettos: Don Giovanni is shown as a petty tyrant, womanizer, chauvinist, and deceiver of his employees and his servant—and he gets his comeuppance at the end. Figaro gets the better of his master, who takes advantage of his servants and employees and all women. In *The Magic Flute,* Mozart casts the Queen of the Night as villainess but displays ambivalence toward this designation by assigning her some of the great arias, although they are arias clearly foreign to the style of the opera as a whole. In *Così,* the audience is motivated to ask whether it is really women, as the characters maintain, or more properly men who are perfidious. In *Magic Flute* and *Entführung,* Mozart finds occasions to spoof racism and ethnocentrism. Gender relationships and identity are questioned: *The Magic Flute* begins with the hero Tamino screaming like a maiden in distress and then being rescued by the "Three Ladies," who sing of triumph in triadic macho martial style, and in *Figaro,* one is left to wonder what kind of person Cherubino is really supposed to be.[19]

Mozart's social criticisms and those of his librettists reside mainly in the plots, the librettos, but they are also part of the music. Thus, the demands made on the singers, and the degree to which spectacular singing is required, are distributed rather equally among the characters. Arguably the most popular section of *Don Giovanni* is the "Catalog Aria," sung by Leporello, the servant. In *Figaro,* the count sings relatively little outstanding music, whereas some of the most memorable arias are given to Cherubino, a minor character whom the count punishes for doing the very things that he has done (or would like to do) himself.

The importance of social criticism in the plots of many of the greatest operas in the hundred years or so after Mozart is noted in a large body of literature. Looking at the librettos of highly popular works as diverse as *Fidelio, Aida, Rigoletto, Meistersinger,* even *Bartered Bride,* and *Wozzeck,* one is struck not only by the critique of central aspects of society, but also by the ways in which the critique is incorporated into a musical style that otherwise reflects a conservative view of society.

Christopher Small asserts that the great prestige of the symphony orchestra and its repertory resides in the degree to which its social structure, as represented in the music, is admired by its audience.[20] Arguing along similar lines, I suggest that opera is admired in large measure because of its complexity, and that the most admired operas present and support a hierarchical social structure (in music, like the orchestra, but as well in drama) while at the same time criticizing it, thus providing a measure of the unpredictable characteristic of great art. Opera is the musical genre of greatest prestige because its works are long and complex—and we view complexity as a major criterion of excellence in art—and also because it exhibits the musico-social structure of conducting-following and soloist-accompanist at several simultaneous levels between major and minor characters, soloists and chorus, singers and orchestra, and conductor and instrumentalists, as well as within the orchestra. Yet at its best, the work of someone like Mozart, its plot, and occasionally its music, contradict the musical world's conventional wisdom.[21]

Like opera, the concerto also epitomizes musical and social values, adding another layer to the already hierarchical social-musical structure of the symphony orchestra and its central repertory. The piano concerto, the most popular variety of the genre, extends the structure by introducing other layers inherent in piano music. Because of its ability to perform as much music as an orchestra and thus function more as a counterbalance to the orchestra than might be the case in violin, cello, or clarinet concertos—to say nothing of its volume—the piano is the concerto instrument par excellence.

Musical and social relationships between piano and orchestra exhibit tensions reminiscent of those described in the ensemble of concerts in Madras. In the social structure of a concert, the piano soloist is in some respects a cut above the conductor and sits between conductor and the audience. On the other hand, judging from the order of entry (concertmaster or mistress, then soloist, then conductor), he or she is inserted into the social structure between conductor and concertmaster. The ambivalence reflects the tension between art as the organization of forces and art as individual accomplishment. The soloist plays alone or is accompanied by the orchestra, takes liberties with tempo, and improvises (or plays music that sounds improvised) in the cadenzas. He or she addresses the audience directly, whereas the orchestra, responding to the soloist, is perhaps no more than a grand accompanying instrument. On the other hand, the history and prehistory of the concerto—the polychoral structure of Baroque works, the Concerto Grosso with its dialogue of concertino and ripieno—support the concept of equal forces in competition and conversation, a concept also suggested by the etymology of the word *concerto*. And so conductor and soloist vie for hegemony in performances of Beethoven's and Mozart's concertos. Sometimes the conductor follows the soloist, watching for nuances and tempo changes and directing the orchestra to follow; at other times, the soloist follows the conductor's beat.

The Priesthood of the Repertory. In Western, particularly American, society, there is tension between the guiding principle of hierarchy and leadership (or, in music, by melody with accompaniment) and the conception of equality of humans. Although humans are distinctly unequal in their resources, abilities, or wealth, society recognizes areas of life in which they are ideally equal, such as the assumption of equal creation upon which American government is founded, or the often-cited equality of all before God. The concept of equality as associated with religion suggests that in the art music repertory we can somehow discover a relationship of equality to sacredness, or to a seriousness suggesting humanity's confrontation with a creator.

Although the solo-and-accompaniment structure is most prominent in the best-loved (but not the most highbrow) portion of the classical repertory, the "priesthood" of the musical repertory seems to appeal most to a part of the audience that considers itself elite. This group highly values the music in which there is textual equality of parts and in which distinctions of power, volume, tone color, and role specialization are relatively unimportant, a body of music that has, in addition to its sonic existence, a life in the abstract. This is music whose structural details play a greater role than the pleasurable nature of its sound, moment to moment. In general, it has no programmatic content and perhaps little in the way of obvious emotional connotations.

This priesthood of the repertory includes genres and forms for which a certain purity is claimed; it is music that plays a major role in the theoretical system and instruction in music theory that govern the learning of the central repertory. Being the music of music theory, it appears also to be the reflection of social theory rather than of social reality. Although Western society is actually based on hierarchies and inequalities of many and conflicting sorts, the theory is that people in this society are equal. In the musical counterpart, if differences in tone color of the orchestra are important to composer and listener because differences in human color (taken narrowly and broadly) make a great difference in society, it is nevertheless the theory that society should be color-blind, and therefore that the music closest to music theory, the most abstract music, also be blind in its use of tone color. The musical genres emphasizing the concept of equality are polyphonic works such as fugues and string quartets, and they appear, in different ways, to function as the Music Building's musical conscience.

Fugue is a form or genre developed to its highest level of perfection by J. S. Bach, whose fugues eventually became totally paradigmatic of the concept; no one else came close—so at least felt later composers. If Mozart and Beethoven are the reigning deities of a music lover's pantheon, and of a performer's, Bach is (or was for two centuries) the composer's composer, an attitude readily documented in the biographies of the great masters from Mozart to Schoenberg.

In music schools, the ability to write fugues was long regarded as the highest accomplishment in the typical theory curriculum. And Bach's system of harmonic selection and progression was the standard for theory courses; it was the technical basic training for musicianship, no matter what the specialty, at American music schools. The entrance examination for graduate study in the Music Building at Heartland U. was for decades a four-part theory affair, with ear training, harmony, and counterpoint as generalized examinations followed by fugue writing and analysis. Further, virtually every piano student had at some point to study "The Well-Tempered Clavier," with its forty-eight fugues. Many later composers paid homage to Bach by composing fugues and placing them in particularly significant locations within their works.

Where a full-fledged fugue was not appropriate, allusion to the fugal principle or a symbolic use of fugato would make the same point. Thus, the last movement of Mozart's Symphony Number 41 begins with fugato. Beethoven's penultimate quartet, Opus 133, is the "Great Fugue," the longest of his quartet movements. Brahms ended his variation sets on themes by Haydn and Handel with fugues. One of Paul Hindemith's major works, "Ludus Tonalis," is a modern reflection of "The Well-Tempered Clavier." Examples are legion, even aside from the use of the fugal principle in organ and choral music. The expression of the serious with the use of fugal or fuguelike structures was an established practice from Mozart. There are many illustrations, from the song of the armed men in *The Magic Flute,* who use it to state the theory of the opera's quasi-Masonic order, to Richard Strauss's *Don Quixote,* which has fuguelike counterpoint representing a band of pilgrims headed for the most sacred of Spanish shrines.

The special role of fugues and imitative counterpoint in twentieth-century art music culture and its discipline seems to result from a combination of technical and social principles. A fugue is very difficult to write, using all of the principles established by Bach, but there are other, perhaps equally difficult genres or styles: the twelve-tone technique in its classic formats, or exercises in Renaissance counterpoint, double-counterpoint, or complex Wagnerian modulations. Yet in important respects the fugue became regarded as the greatest technical accomplishment of composer's craft long after the great fugues of Bach had been composed.

The fugues by Bach, or in Bach's style, have the quality of sacred texts. As an exercise in equality, avoiding the musical replication of social structure that the solo-plus-accompaniment in all of its complex and varied manifestations provides, fugue has a certain purity because the composer can write outside the confines of the musical representations of social or political constraints, in the abstract, and in musical spirit without musical body. Fugues usually are not intended to provide a variety of moods and are hardly used programmatically except to suggest the serious. Fugue has become associated with

Christianity and its disciplines and serves as a sign of unchanging values, of composers' allegiance to the roots of the classic. Fugues are conceived as musical structure in a quintessential sense, admitting (or at least requiring) no variations of tempo, dynamics, tone color, and harmonic style. The special qualities and competencies of different instruments are not brought into play because all of the voices of a fugue have identical tasks; they are the humans who are equal before God.

The purity, religiosity, and seriousness of fugues is matched by the social contexts in which fugues typically appear. In church, fugues may be performed alone; in the concert culture, they are presented only as parts—but usually the climactic or most serious parts—of other, larger works. In the society of musicians, and in the society of musics and musical works, fugues are thus treated quite differently from other genres.

Like fugues, string quartets also exude seriousness and are rarely written to express nonmusical ideas, describe events, or show off string technique. Unlike orchestra (with its symphonies, overtures, and tone poems) or piano (with sonatas, short pieces, and fantasias), the quartet is not simply an ensemble serving as medium for a variety of genres. The repertory (up to around 1970) is almost entirely works titled "String Quartet," each requiring from twenty-five to forty-five minutes. In contrast to the ritual structure of symphony concerts, quartet concerts most commonly consist of three works (all titled "Quartet"), each with three or four movements, the intermission after the second, the earliest work usually first, and the largest, last.

The concept of equality can be observed from several angles. The three works in a concert are relatively equal compared to the obvious hierarchy of works in a symphony concert. Less superficial is the equality of the four instrumental voices. Like fugues, quartets are "pure" musical thought and structure, typically avoiding instrumental or compositional virtuosity for the exclusive purpose of showing off. (But this does not mean that they may not be exceedingly difficult to play.) The concept of solo with accompaniment is mitigated as each instrument takes its turn as soloist, as contrapuntal structures play a major role, and as the solo instrument of the moment is not set off by its unique tone color. To be sure, the earliest important quartets (by Franz Joseph Haydn) feature the first violin accompanied by the rest, but all major composers, from Mozart, Beethoven, and Schubert through Brahms and Verdi, to Schoenberg and Bartók, tried their hands at quartets, and the equality of the four instruments intensified.

In the Music Building, one senses the belief that fugues and string quartets are art music in a greater and purer sense than are other genres, that they are, in a sense, the "conscience" of the music world. This concept is underscored by their special treatment in the Music Building. Although few schools can actually carry out the intention, most would like to have a university organist and a quartet in residence. The concept of "university organist" goes back to the early, church-related years of many colleges. And yet even in the 1950s and later, organists were central figures in the musical life of institutions. The notion that hearing string quartet concerts is an indispensable experience for music students—more so than hearing orchestra concerts, piano recitals, piano trio concerts, or, for that matter, operas or gamelan concerts—is wide-spread. Fugues and quartets are, more than other genres, the music of musicians par excellence.

Fuges and string quartets are, in the Music Building and in the institutions associated with it, music of the older generation. Audiences at quartet concerts are older than average concert audiences; most members are middle-aged or elderly, and there are few students. (But members of string quartets are often quite young.) Events comprised largely of fugues, most frequently organ recitals plus the occasional piano recital featuring "The Well-Tempered Clavier" or "Ludus Tonalis," are likewise attended more by middle-aged and older persons. This is the serious music of the society, the music associated with eternal and spiritual values, with discipline of the mind, music that eschews the worldly values that result in social inequalities. Virtually all composers in the period that produced the central repertory, whatever their specialties, tried their hand at fugues and quartets.

Do denizens of the Music Building really think of the genres and pieces of music in their repertories as a family? Would they talk about Daddy Jupiter, Grandpa Ninth, Cousin Phantasie Opus 17, and Well-Tempered Auntie with Holy Orders? Of course, my association of the two structures is a theoretical abstraction, an interpretation supported more by musical than by verbal practice. If we can take social structure to be the heart of culture, as classic social anthropologists such as Radcliffe-Brown suggest, and if the way people relate to each other is fundamental to economic and political structures, as suggested by Marvin Harris or, when it comes to music, by such scholars as Alan Lomax, then it may make sense to look at other domains in culture as reflections of social organization, of the way people in a society interact.[22] And, following Daniel M. Neuman, if music is a microcosm of culture and one of its tasks is to comment on the culture of which it is a part, it is reasonable to suggest that Americans in the Music Building, a building ruled by deceased deities, use their music—especially the music composed in the rather distant past—as a way of expressing their comments on society and culture.[23] Their musical actions, if not their words, interpret this repertory's structure as somewhat like society's as they perceive it—a social organization driven by classes and inequities, but with the theory that all are created equal.

Cultural Performance

Prelude: The Grand Powwow

The grand annual powwow that takes place on the Blackfeet Indian Reservation in Browning, Montana, around July 10 has many purposes, but one is surely the desire to locate the Blackfoot people and their culture in the broader social environment in which they live. In its various aspects, it shows to the Blackfoot people themselves, and to others who attend, that this is a culture with a unique history and a unique present; that the Blackfoot in Montana associate closely with Blackfoot people in Canada and elsewhere; that they are part of a broad-based contemporary Native American culture; that they are part of the American West; and that they have a definite if ambivalent feeling of being Americans in the social and political sense. The North American Indian Days powwow annually reminds everyone of these ties and thus qualifies, in the technical sense of the term, as a "cultural performance."[24]

Since 1970, a number of works have appeared in which a ritual is presented as cultural performance in great detail and play-by-play description and then is shown to be a synthesis of cultural values. In ethnomusicology, Anthony Seeger, Regula Qureshi, Christopher Small, Daniel Neuman, Ruth Stone, and Henry Kingsbury have provided studies that in various ways see musical events as "cultural performance" or as rites of passage.[25] In academic life, a commencement may fill both functions; it moves people into a new stage of life and, while doing so, reminds them of the culture's (or subculture's) principal values.

The Commencement

The ethnomusicologist from the distant planet is taken to an event described as one of the really important occasions in the music school's academic year: the commencement celebrating the graduation of the school's seniors and master's and doctor's candidates. Some two hundred people in black mortarboards and gowns had been milling around, and the dominant decorative color is the light pink of hoods, tassels, and chevron-derived stripes. The people march to the front of the auditorium to the strains of a work that is being played that same Sunday at hundreds of other graduations, seat and ready themselves for an hour of celebration and, so some members imply by their whispers, boredom. The program turns out to be rather short. A priest prays briefly, the head of the school speaks for three minutes, then a distinguished professor of composition at greater length, and finally one of the graduating students speaks. A short piece by a brass ensemble punctuates the event, and then the graduates march across the stage, each receiving a folder to hold his or her diploma. Cursory announcements of awards and retirements precede the exodus of faculty, graduates, and the delighted relatives to the strains of another faster but familiar piece. Outside the auditorium, the crowd gives itself over to an orgy of congratulatory hugging and photography. This is an account of one commencement at Heartland U.; on other occasions and in other years, the course of events was similar but not identical. The main outlines and the principal characteristics have remained, however.

Commencements are a familiar secular ritual in North America, the most important rite of passage in academic life, and the event has analogues in Europe and elsewhere. It may also be seen as a cultural performance for the members of Music Building society, who enact it in order to confirm their principal values and define their place in broader society. Commencements should be considered in greater detail to see what they reveal about the values of music, about musical values, and about the way these relate to cultural values at large. There are explicit and implied statements.

A Celebration of Art Music. For one thing, commencements celebrate Western art music, particularly its central repertory. Whatever other kinds of music may have occasionally been the concern of the graduates, these are not allowed to play a role. The graduates spent most of their time studying classical music, but some were also active as jazz, rock, or country musicians. Commencement makes it clear that primary allegiance to art music is virtually a requirement for membership in Music Building society. Accordingly, the purpose of commencements is in part to extol art music, more implicitly than explicitly.

This is clearly the intention of the establishment, of administration and faculty, of old grads and benefactors, and probably of most students as well. But there is nevertheless a familiar tension among values. For example, the graduates and the students take for granted but are also mildly embarrassed to be in a school that might well be named "School of Western European Classical Music." The students are, after all, from a segment of society that takes a degree of affluence for granted, knowing it to be virtually essential for success in the music of this school. To be at the top, even in a music school context, brings the expectation of a top-notch instrument, and who could afford to hit up her parents for a $10,000 flute or a $15,000 cello? Some students feel that this unjust state of affairs is inappropriate because they have also absorbed the concept that equality should be basic to the society they inhabit. They question the justice of something that has been drummed into their heads since their early childhood; they are not totally happy in thinking, "I am a better person because I practice Beethoven and (most of the time, at least) eschew rock, country, reggae, pop, and what not else, and have avoided becoming polluted." It seems to me, however, that at commencement these caveats are laid aside, and art music itself is celebrated for its specialness, along with the degrees.

Priesthood to Celebrate, Army to Defend. That the commencement is a celebration of art music is made explicit in some of the addresses. The head of the school tells the audience that music is worthwhile, that students should be applauded for having selected it as a field of study, and that works of music are among the greatest creations of humanity. It is clear that the head means "humanity in Western culture"— works of size and complexity, reflections of our athletic view of music, and works that require enormous effort of musical technology, forces, and concentration such as Bach's B Minor Mass, Wagner's *Meistersinger,* and Beethoven's last quartets. The way that the word *works* is used in the rhetoric indicates this attitude.

The professor of composition begins by listing the kinds of music that there are in the school: jazz, commercial musics of many kinds, non-Western music, early music, folk music, church music, and then two special categories, art music and contemporary music. The professor says that the last two are the ones to which the graduates ought to devote themselves, because these categories require special nurturing. The other music can take care of itself, but without special support—training, practice, criticism, and patronage—art music and contemporary art music cannot survive. The implication is that although all musics may have their places in culture, graduates should see themselves as a priesthood for the preservation and practice of art music and contemporary art music and also for their development.

On this highly significant day, the taxonomy of music, and the hierarchy it embodies, is presented to the graduates, perhaps explicitly for the first time and with emphasis. It is hard to know how often they have discussed this taxonomy during their student days, but I would guess that it did not come up frequently. It has been taken for granted, and the composer's presentation of it and of its role in the graduates' lives at commencement is rather like an initiation. One might almost think that the graduates are finally being told why they have been studying a particular repertory so hard: to become priests of the elite music.

The student speaker, following the professorial teacher's thoughts and restating them with more emphasis, exhorts graduates to become missionaries by playing, composing, teaching, and researching the great art music. That term—*art music*—is actually not used, but others—*masterwork, greatness, difficulty, innovation,* and a smattering of genre names—*oratorio, opera,* and *symphony*—make clear the frame of reference. The commencement is not a required event, and there are, no doubt, graduates who don't show up, who disagree with the music school's values and don't care to hear them extolled, and so we should avoid overstressing commencement's importance among the year's events. But its explicit presentation of the values of the institution—in contrast to many events at which their presentation is only implied—gives it a special significance.

Along with the initiation of the graduates into a priesthood whose task it is to missionize, to promulgate art music and urge society to replace other kinds of music with it, there is also a subtext. Its implied focus is that graduates should be an army willing to defend a beleaguered position because art music appears constantly to be losing ground to other kinds of music in the school's taxonomy. Some speakers mentioned the degree to which the maintenance of art music is threatened by lack of financial and governmental support; by the increasing willingness of graduates to make their living by playing rock and country music or becoming studio musicians for the mass media; by the dilution of art music as it is quoted and parodied in television commercials and popular songs; by lack of a truly appreciative audience; by trivializing as was done by the "Mozart industry" and the dissemination of excerpt records; and by decreased attention in the public schools.[26] One hears expressions of fear. The job of the graduates is to work at the reversal of these trends. Good music must be defended, its study justified.

The student speaker warns graduates that their choice of an art music career will be greeted with wonder and perhaps derision by friends who go into presumably more lucrative fields such as engineering and commerce (a groundless worry, I think). The graduates are told several times that musicians should consider themselves fortunate to have succeeded in this art whose practice provides greater joy than that of other fields, although worldly rewards may not be forthcoming. The special sacredness of music, ruled by the pantheon of great masters, is presented throughout, if only by circumlocution. There is a feeling that the believers must be reconfirmed in belief and resolve.

The aspect of the classical music that this army is being asked to defend is mainly its emphasis on faith in the status quo, internal consistency, and love of the old days, but not the emphasis of radical innovation. It is thus an approach to the musical scene that depicts Mozart as its conservative cornerstone, the universal norm of music, the pinnacle at which music forever would have satisfied the world's audience (representing a social system that could also have been maintained forever). It is a view that neglects to remind us of Mozart's other side, forgetting that some of his greatest works are literally and musically sharply critical of social injustices, inequality of classes and genders, and brutalities such as duels and racism.

The Color Pink. Another side of the subtext of defensiveness concerns the symbolism of color at commencements. Recipients of music degrees wear pink academic hoods, sometimes pink chevrons on their doctoral gowns, and pink tassels on their mortarboards. Not all of them are happy with this choice of color, and their ambivalence has something to do with classical musicians' belief that they must defend their position, must struggle for survival of their profession and their art. They fear that they will inevitably suffer from the residue of the centuries-old subordinate role of musicians in Western and other cultures. Here the commencement provides a microcosm of the way American society broadly assigns the roles of its major domains. Music in America does not itself have a subordinate role; no one can imagine life without it. But it is (or has been) associated with the subordinate social classes and subcultures symbolized by the color pink.

Other than the expression "in the pink," the color is associated with baby girls, by extension with women generally, and sometimes, by further extension, with male homosexuals. In the period after 1945, the color was also associated with liberals and socialists ("pinkos"). Was the assignment of pink as the color of the hoods for music degrees simply a coincidence, the fact that many colors had been taken when the degrees began to be recognized in the academy and dignified with caps and gowns? When colors were distributed, did someone blurt out unthinking, "Pink, of course, what kinds of people get these degrees, anyway?" The system of colors was established for the United States at a conference at Columbia University in 1895, but I find no account of the debates that must have accompanied the event.[27]

In their ultimate origins, academic colors may go back to medieval universities, where pink, salmon, or red were associated with music for totally different reasons.[28] But in late twentieth-century America, pink connotes a particular population. There is some historical background for this. Music departments were first developed in women's colleges, women made up the bulk—if not the leadership—of the musical population, and music was one occupation in which homosexuality was widely tolerated and in which various kinds of unconventional behavior symbolized by long-haired musicians and by political and social radicals were stock in trade. Society at large may think pink is the right color for music, but many academic musicians do not. Conversations with staff members of Collegiate Cap and Gown Company in Champaign, Illinois, one of the leading manufacturers and distributors, indicate that a good many musicians are unhappy with their color.

Art and Power

The principal text of the commencement is pride in and promulgation of the elite music; the subtext is fear of ostracism and the need to defend. This is clear. Yet there is another, more puzzling, aspect of the value complex being presented to the graduates, one related to the two ways of identifying the culture's central music, the greatest as against the music central to the major rituals. The great composer-deities are obviously present. Their inscribed names adorn the building inside and out, six masters (four of them German) instructing students assembled for weekly convocations in the auditorium that all important issues of music reside within a 150-year span and nothing else is needed—this is the great music. But if graduates are being initiated into a life of service to these great composers, the music they hear at commencement is not by them. Instead, one hears second-rank composers: The organ plays a work by Edward Elgar for entering and one by Charles-Marie Widor for departure. A brass quintet movement by Vaclav Nelhybel is a punctuating number, while the audience was entertained before the procession by a bassoon ensemble.

In this society, the greatest art is string and keyboard (and possibly vocal) music by the great German composers, but it is the winds, principally brass, that represent political power, usually music by composers of other nationalities. We have seen the equation of art with strings, politics and war with winds, in Western and other cultures and made the analogy of this structure with the political class structure of music faculties. Commencements, although at a modest artistic level, are high in their power component. Not just high-class entertainment, commencements actually moves people through the hoops of society and thus require performance by the politically powerful wind instruments.

Although the event I have described is only one of hundreds of commencements that could have been studied and is surely not totally representative, its use of wind music by non-Germans, performed largely by men (although a slight majority of the graduates and audience is comprised of women) was probably not coincidental. As the graduates broke ranks, joined parents and favorite teachers, took myriads of pictures, and went off to imbibe countless glasses of orange-colored punch, they were perhaps not aware that they had just participated in an event in which the principal values of the Western musical world, their relationship to social values at large, and some of the conflicts among these values had been exhibited and taken out of storage bins for annual exercise.

Afterword

Having tried to play my three roles, I must now ask myself whether I have provided and used credible information; whether my own experience is representative; whether I found reliable handles on the culture, presented the Heartland music schools in such a way that its denizens would recognize themselves, and gave a reasonably sympathetic view. Someone else must provide the answers, but readers should be aware of my own trepidation in trying to look at the culture in which I live.

Henry Kingsbury, in a discussion that is specifically focussed on one conservatory not part of a major university but nevertheless with much in common with the Heartland music schools, has tried to accomplish, although with somewhat different approaches and emphases, what I have also attempted here.[1] Readers will note similarities and differences, but Kingsbury deals more with processes and I more with structures; he is more concerned with the politics of relationships involving power, and I more with the formal reflections of social, educational, and musical relationships.

The impression Kingsbury has given to some readers is of a culture or subculture that is essentially mean and even brutish to most of its population. Ellen Koskoff's review suggests that Kingsbury has "an axe to grind"; that he wishes to "laugh, poke fun at, or cry . . . at the grim reality of conservatory life"; and that he will only convince those musicians "who remember their own musical training with resentment and who want, deep down, to settle the score."[2] Kingsbury does not totally deny these aims in his response, because he closes his rejoinder by citing Howard Becker to the effect that social scientists must make judgments and that "appeals for 'balanced' accounts in the social sciences are all too often merely veiled admonitions to endorse the status quo."[3] Kingsbury would presumably like to see change in the conservatory, change that would improve life and maybe improve music, and I applaud and agree. Even the rosiest picture would have to contain its share of grimness. And so I, too, would like to see change, although at this point I am not sure from what to what.

It's a complicated place, the Heartland music school, existing as it does at a number of crossroads. It's a place that aims specifically to teach a set of values, and it does so not only through practical instruction but also through the presentation of a quasi-religious system. It's a place that puts "the music" first and looks at music as if it were a reflection of a homogeneous human society. It is an umbrella under which different approaches to music can coexist, interact, and argue. It collects many kinds of music, brought from many places and composed at many different times, putting them all under one roof but making them all march to the drummer of the central classical tradition. It reflects the culture in which it lives, but it also tries to direct that culture in certain directions. It mediates between music as a participating constituent part of culture and music as the domain of the foreign and unintelligible.

However, I have tried to avoid endorsing anything. If an explicitly critical stance will preach only to the converted, then perhaps an approach that tries to present a balanced picture might show champions of the status quo why they should depart from it. But that will have to be their own choice. An article of faith with most ethnomusicologists is that they should try their best to avoid disturbing the cultures they study or introducing new musics and practices, and that they should also restrain themselves from unduly encouraging musical cultures to eschew change in order to preserve the past. And, in my role of ethnomusicologist, I wish to abide by this principle, even when considering the culture in which I live. As much as I can.

But still, we have this—by many criteria—great music, styles, and genres that have been accepted in most of the world as music at its best. Yet this music lives and is transmitted in institutions that abound in conflict and inequality, in which population groups and their musical surrogates constantly jockey for position, in which little is said that does not make comparative evaluations and where everyone keeps score. A critical observer might wish to ask whether music schools have to be this way. And, I would add, What is it about Western culture that makes this great music so representative of aspects of our cultural system with which many denizens of the music school would not wish to be identified? It is not a trivial question, and I suspect that many ethnomusicologists whose background is in the Western classical tradition have agonized over it. Indeed, perhaps the invention of ethnomusicology could take place only in a society that constantly negotiates between ethnocentrism (and musical ethnocentrism), which I take to be part of the nature of culture, and cultural (and musical) relativism, which we can espouse but rarely accomplish.

And so I am unable to explain to my own satisfaction why the values and structures of the Heartland music school reflect certain ones of contemporary American culture while they seem at the same time to contradict some of its ideals. It may all have to do with the anomalous position of music in our society and in many societies: The musician is a stranger, but music is needed and loved, although sometimes feared. Music is closely associated with our conception of the supernatural, but it also reflects human relationships and the human condition both explicitly and abstractly. The music school is the analogue of factory, corporation, and scientific establishment; it reflects the society of which it is a part. But if music came into existence, as some believe, as a special language with which humans could speak to God, or to the gods, then its institutions may also maintain a position of standing outside the culture, contradicting, approving, debating, and commenting.

Notes

Introduction

1. Christopher Small, "Performance as Ritual: Sketch for an Enquiry into the Nature of a Symphony Concert," in *Lost in Music: Culture, Style, and the Musical Event,* ed. Avron Levine White (London: Routledge and Kegan Paul, 1987), 6–23; Judith Becker, "Is Western Art Music Superior?" *Musical Quarterly* 72 (1986): 341–59; Catherine Cameron, "Dialectics in the Arts: Composer Ideology and Culture Change," Ph.D. diss., University of Illinois at Urbana–Champaign, 1982; Pierre Bourdieu, *Distinction: A Social Critique of the Judgment of Taste,* trans. Richard Nice (Cambridge: Harvard University Press, 1984); Ruth Finnegan, *The Hidden Musicians: Music-Making in an English Town* (Cambridge: Cambridge University Press, 1989); Henry Kingsbury, *Music, Talent, and Performance: A Conservatory Cultural System* (Philadelphia: Temple University Press, 1988). A publication of particular relevance is *Community of Music: An Ethnographic Seminar in Champaign-Urbana,* ed. Tamara E. Livingston et al. (Champaign: Elephant and Cat, 1993).

The ways in which my book parallels Kingsbury's will become obvious, as will the divergent ways in which I have chosen to describe and interpret some similar or even identical structures and processes. Kingsbury is more specifically devoted to one institution, whereas I am trying to look at a type. Kingsbury's approach is more critical than mine, which attempts to maintain a nonjudgmental attitude. Kingsbury provides many anecdotal illustrations, whereas I have been more inclined to look at structures. More concretely, Kingsbury's Eastern Metropolitan Conservatory is an independent institution in a major city, whereas the midwestern schools of music with which I am concerned are in smaller cities or college towns but are components of large universities with whose other parts they interact. Kingsbury is concerned with certain central concepts, such as talent, around which he builds his work; I am trying to pass through the institutions four times in somewhat distinct ways. I have avoided referring to Kingsbury at every possible opportunity, and I will compare what I say with his statements only on a few occasions, including in the Afterword. I wish to express my appreciation and admiration of Kingsbury's work, which has been helpful, influential, and stimulating as I formulated my own observations.

2. To be sure, ethnomusicology has no monopoly on breadth of perspective. Thoughtful interpretation, taking into consideration the cultural position of the observer, has characterized much work in historical and systematic musicology for a century. In the period since 1980, influenced to some extent by developments in ethnomusicology and anthropology, music historians have begun to move closer to positions often considered quintessentially ethnomusicological. The literature is extensive; see Joseph Kerman, *Contemplating Music: Challenges to Musicology* (Cambridge: Harvard University Press, 1985); Rose Subotnick, *Developing Variations: Style and Ideology in Western Music* (Minneapolis: University of Minnesota Press, 1991); and *Disciplining Music: Musicology and Its Canons,* ed. Katherine Bergeron and Philip V. Bohlman (Chicago: University of Chicago Press, 1992).

3. I have drawn insight from these seminars and from resulting essays published in *Community of Music,* ed. Livingston et al., particularly Colin Franey, "Composers' Forum: A Compositional Taste-Test"; Mi-yon Kim, "Musical Organizations in an Ethnic Student Group: The Korean Church Choir and the Samulnori Pae"; Eunmi Shim, "Taking Lessons and Practicing: The Piano and Tuba Cultures in the School of Music"; Tamara E. Livingston, "Rehearsals and Academic Music-Making: The Russian Folk Orchestra and the University Symphony"; Lise Waxer, "Just Hangin' Out and Playing Guitar: Music and Individualism"; Patricia Sandler, "Aspects of Women's Life in the School of Music: Pedagogy, Sexualization, Identity"; Melinda Russell, "Undergraduate Conceptions of Music"; and Craig Macrae, "Integrating a Society: Persian Music in the Iranian Community."

4. Ruth Benedict, *Patterns of Culture* (Boston: Houghton Mifflin, 1934).

5. Bronislaw Malinowski, *Argonauts of the Western Pacific* (London: Routledge, 1922), 24–25.

6. Clifford Geertz, "Deep Play: Notes on the Balinese Cockfight," *Daedalus* 101 (1972): 1–37 (reprinted in several anthologies).

7. Claude Lévi-Strauss's best-known work along these lines in English translation is *The Raw and the Cooked: Introduction to the Science of Mythology* (New York: Harper and Row, 1969). See also Steven Feld, *Sound and Sentiment* (Philadelphia: University of Pennsylvania Press, 1982).

8. Daniel M. Neuman, *The Life of Music in North India* (Detroit: Wayne State University Press, 1980).

9. Alan P. Merriam, *Ethnomusicology of the Flathead Indians* (Chicago: Aldine Press, 1967).

10. Anthony Seeger, *Why Suyá Sing* (Cambridge: Cambridge University Press, 1988).

11. James Clifford, *The Predicament of Culture: Twentieth-Century Ethnography, Literature, and Art* (Cambridge: Harvard University Press, 1988), 46–54.

12. For more commentary on this question, see Bruno Nettl, *The Study of Ethnomusicology: Twenty-nine Issues and Concepts* (Urbana: University of Illinois Press, 1983), 234–41.

13. Neuman, *The Life of Music in North India,* 27–29.

14. Alan P. Merriam, "Basongye Musicians and Institutionalized Social Deviance," *Yearbook of the International Folk Music Council* 11 (1979): 1–26, provides a detailed analysis of one example. See also Merriam's *The Anthropology of Music* (Evanston: Northwestern University Press, 1964), 138–42. My references in this book to relevant bibliography are selective rather than comprehensive.

Chapter 1: In the Service of the Masters

1. Walter Wiora, *Das musikalische Kunstwerk* (Tutzing: Hans Schneider, 1983).

2. John Spitzer, "Musical Attribution and Critical Judgment: The Rise and Fall of the Sinfonia Concertante for Winds, K. 297b," *Journal of Musicology* 5 (1987): 321.

3. A study exemplifying this approach is Rita Steblin, "The Newly Discovered Hochenecker Portrait of Beethoven (1819): 'Das ähnlichste Bildnis Beethovens,'" *Journal of the American Musiclogical Society* 45 (1992): 468–94.

4. For commentary on the list of composers at Harvard University and its genesis, see Elliot Forbes, *A History of Music at Harvard to 1972* (Cambridge: Harvard University Department of Music, 1988), 57.

5. For a graphic commentary on the canon of great composers and their busts on the piano, see the dust jacket of *Disciplining Music: Musicology and Its Canons,* ed. Katherine Bergeron and Philip V. Bohlman (Chicago: University of Chicago Press, 1992), especially in relationship to the contents of the book, and also the chapter by Don Randel.

6. It is said (although I cannot vouch for the authenticity of the story) that one European-born retired professor of music at one Heartland U. left the music achool, as an heirloom, a portion of Beethoven's skull. It was accepted gratefully and put in storage, although no one has attempted to authenticate it or determine how it may have come into the professor's possession.

7. Wolfgang Hildesheimer, *Mozart,* trans. Marion Faber (New York: Vintage Books, 1983), 366; Alfred Einstein, *Mozart, His Character, His Work* (London: Oxford University Press, 1945), 103.

8. Ian Crofton and Donald Fraser, *A Dictionary of Musical Quotations* (New York: Schirmer Books, 1985).

9. Nicolas Slonimsky, *Baker's Biographical Dictionary of Musicians,* 6th ed. (New York: Schirmer, 1978), 1197, 126.

10. See the discussion of Grove's views, and of other nineteenth-century comparisons of Schubert and Beethoven, in David Gramit, "Constructing a Victorian Schubert: Music, Biography, and Cultural Values," *Nineteenth Century Music* 17 (1993): 65–78.

11. See the account of the "Schubertiade" of New York, January 1992, held at the 92d Street Y in Joseph Horowitz, "Schubert: Eternally Feminine?" *New York Times,* Jan. 19, 1992, H27. See also Lawrence Kramer, ed., "Schubert: Music, Sexuality, Culture," special issue of *Nineteenth Century Music* 17, no. 1 (1993).

12. See, for example, Susan McClary, *Feminine Endings: Music, Gender, and Sexuality* (Minneapolis: University of Minnesota Press, 1991), 18, 69.

13. For an example of this kind of analysis, see Alexander L. Ringer, "Ende gut alles gut: Bemerkungen zu zwei Finalsätzen von Johannes Brahms und Gustav Mahler," in *Neue Musik und Tradition: Festschrift Rudolf Stephan,* ed. Josef Kuckertz (Laaber: Laaber-Verlag, 1990), 297–309.

14. John H. Mueller, *The American Symphony Orchestra: A Social History of Musical Taste* (Bloomington: Indiana University Press, 1951), 182–229.

15. Henry Kingsbury, *Music, Talent, and Performance: A Consrvatory Cultural System* (Philadelphia: Temple University Press, 1988), 59–83.

16. Peter Shaffer, *Amadeus* (New York: Harper and Row, 1980).

17. For a historical and critical discussion of the issues involved in historical and authentic performance and performance-practice, see Joseph Kerman, *Contemplating Music Challenges to Musicology* (Cambridge: Harvard University Press, 1985), 182–214.

18. The wide-ranging role of a figure such as Mozart in everyday life and its polysemic character are made clear through the many essays in Peter Csobádi et al., eds. *Das Phänomen Mozart im 20. Jahrhundert: Wirkung, Verarbeitung und Vermarktung in Literatur, bildender Kunst und in den Medien* (Anif/Salzburg: Ursula Müller-Speiser, 1991). Also see Marshall Brown, "Mozart and After: The Revolution in Musical Consumerism," *Critical Inquiry* 7, no. 4 (1980): 689–94, and many articles in the press around 1991, for example, Richard Taruskin, "Why Mozart Has Become an Icon for Today," *New York Times,* Sept. 9, 1990, H35, H40.

19. James R. Oestreich, "'Mr. Mozart' Comes to Lincoln Center," *New York Times,* Jan. 20, 1991, H1, 30 (about Neal Zaslaw).

20. In his book *Sound and Sentiment* (Philadelphia: University of Pennsylvania Press, 1982), Steven Feld explains the musical culture of the Kaluli people of New Guinea by analysis of a myth about a boy who became a bird; the approach owes much to the work of Claude Lévi-Strauss.

21. My account of the elaborate Blackfoot myth is synthesized from several published versions, most important is the summary in John C. Ewers, *The Blackfeet: Raiders on the Northwestern Plains* (Norman: University of Oklahoma Press, 1958), 168–69.

22. Beaverman is so named in a compendium of Blackfoot mythology by a Blackfoot author, Percy Bullchild, *The Sun Came Down* (New York: Harper and Row, 1985).

23. For a sampling of presentations of Mozart and, to a smaller degree, Beethoven materials for children, see Kenneth McLeish and Valerie McLeish, *The Oxford First Companion to Music* (London: Oxford University Press, 1982), F14; Ian McLean, *Mozart* (London: Hamlin, 1990); Ian Woodward, *Lives of the Great Composers* (Loughborough: Wills and Hepworth, 1969), 1:20–34; and Benjamin Britten and Imogen Holst, *The Wonderful World of Music* (Garden City: Doubleday, 1958), 42–43. For a slightly more adult approach, see Bruno Rauch, "Verehrt und vermarktet," *Coop-Zeitung* (Basel), July 18, 1991, 38–43. I am grateful to my colleague Eve Harwood for information on children's materials. Further, see Csobádi et al., eds., *Das Phänomen Mozart;* for a different and earlier perspective, see Edith Sterba and Richard Sterba, *Beethoven and His Nephew* (New York: Pantheon, 1954) and Alessandra Comini, *The Changing Image of Beethoven: A Study in Myth-Making* (New York: Rizzoli, 1987).

24. Gustav Becking, *Der musikalische Rhytmus als Erkenntnisquelle* (Augsburg: B. Filser, 1928). For more recent work along somewhat related lines, see Alan Lomax et al., *Folk Song Style and Culture* (Washington: American Association for the Advancement of Science, 1968).

25. See Joseph Kerman, *Listen,* 2d ed. (New York: Worth, 1976); Curt Sachs, *Our Musical Heritage* (New York: Prentice-Hall, 1948); and K. Marie Stolba, *The Development of Western Music: A History* (Dubuque: Wm. C. Brown, 1990) for examples of textbooks in which this kind of classification plays a role. Sachs especially makes use of it in his headings. In my undergraduate experience, it was the normal mnemonic device for remembering and associating composers.

26. Alan P. Merriam, *The Anthropology of Music* (Evanston: Northwestern University Press, 1964), 85–86.

27. Alice Urbach, *So kocht man in Wien* (Vienna: Zentralgesellschaft für buchwerbliche und graphische Betriebe, 1936).

28. Bonnie Wade, *Music in India: The Classical Traditions* (Englewood Cliffs: Prentice-Hall, 1979), 78.

29. It is true that the Mozart-Beethoven contrast is often used as a paradigm of important distinctions in the world of conceptions surrounding Western art music. But the degree to which Mozart is the source of symbolism greatly exceeds that of Beethoven, as suggested by the large number of essays in Csobádi et al., eds., *Das Phänomen Mozart*. In the Beethoven years, 1970 and 1977, there was nothing like the amount of attention given to Mozart in 1991. Comparison is difficult and inhibited by changes in politics, the role of mass media, and economic matters, but the facts that Mozart seems (as far as we are concerned—don't forget, this has nothing to do with what really happened in the eighteenth century) more susceptible to humorous depiction and characterization than Beethoven, and that his music virtually defines the norms of Western music and is even, on the surface, "easier listening," may both play a role.

30. Anthony Burgess, *A Clockwork Orange* (New York: Ballantine, 1963), and *The End of the World News* (New York: McGraw-Hill, 1983).

31. Bruno Nettl, *The Radif of Persian Music,* rev. ed. (Champaign: Elephant and Cat, 1987), 3–5, 104, 165.

32. Nettl, *The Radif of Persion Music,* 184–92.

33. Bruno Nettl, *Blackfoot Musical Thought: Comparative Perspectives* (Kent: Kent State University Press, 1989), 137–40.

34. For the beginnings of a bibliography, with all its available variety, see Leonard B. Meyer, *Music, the Arts, and Ideas: Patterns and Predictions in Twentieth-Century Culture* (Chicago: University of Chicago Press, 1967); Charles Seeger, "Music and Class Structure in the United States," *American Quarterly* 9 (1957): 281–94; Christopher Small, "Performance as Ritual: Sketch for an Enquiry into the Nature of a Symphony Concert," in *Lost in Music: Culture, Style, and the Musical Event,* ed. Avron Levine White (London: Routledge and Kegan Paul, 1987); Rose Subotnick, *Developing Variations: Style and Ideology in Western Music* (Minneapolis: University of Minnesota Press, 1991); and Kingsbury, *Music, Talent, and Performance.*

35. This is discussed by many authors, from Theodor W. Adorno, *Introduction to the Sociology of Music,* trans. E. B. Ashton (New York: Continuum, 1976), 104–17, to Small, "Performance as Ritual," 17–18.

36. For elaboration of this theme, see Elias Canetti, *Crowds and Power,* trans. Carol Stewart (New York: Viking Press, 1962), 394–96.

37. E. D. Hirsch, Jr., *Cultural Literacy: What Every American Needs to Know* (Boston: Houghton Mifflin, 1987), 10–18.

38. In *Music, Talent, and Performance,* Kingsbury discusses with considerable emphasis this opposition between "music" and "notes" and the difference between "musical" and "technical" issues, despite the fact that the word for notated pieces in this culture is simply *music;* see in particular chapters 4 and 6.

39. This has long been understood implicitly by ethnomusicologists, who have usually given considerable attention to transmission processes, culture by culture, but the matter has not often been synthesized interculturally. See, however, Merriam, *The Anthropology of Music*, ch. 8; Bruno Nettl, *The Study of Ethnomusicology: Twenty-nine Issues and Concepts* (Urbana: University of Illinois Press, 1983), ch. 25; and, for a treatment from the perspective of music education, Patricia Shehan Campbell, *Lessons from the World* (New York: Schirmer Books, 1991).

40. Curt Sachs, *Our Musical Heritage* (New York: Prentice-Hall, 1948), 378.

41. Richard Schaal, "Konzertwesen" in *Die Musik in Geschichte und Gegenwart,* ed. Friedrich Blume (Kassel: Bärenreiter, 1958), 7:1589, 1597.

42. Despite the widespread use of relatively standard patterns, the construction of a program is a matter that receives much attention from performers, who regard it very much a personal matter. For a sample of a personal statement, see Alfred Brendel, "The Pianist and the Program," *New York Review of Books,* Nov. 22, 1990, 35–36.

43. Mueller, *The American Symphony Orchestra*, 183–209.

44. This was not only the case in 1991, as indicated by Csobádi et al., eds., *Das Phänomen Mozart,* or because of the fictional works by Shaffer and his predecessors, but even in the scholarly literature, as indicated by the tone in Hildesheimer, *Mozart,* and earlier, as in the selections in Alfred Orel, *Mozart: Gloria Mundi* (Salzburg: Ludwig Schäffer, 1956). It is nevertheless noteworthy that the greatest gestures of worship appear at times of greatest ceremonial significance, such as centenaries.

Chapter 2: Society of Musicians

1. For commentary on social interrelationship of Carnatic musicians, see Kathleen l'Armand and Adrian l'Armand, "Music in Madras: The Urbanization of a Cultural Tradition" in *Eight Urban Musical Cultures,* ed. Bruno Nettl (Urbana: University of Illinois Press, 1978), 115–45.

2. It is tempting to use the terminology of earlier sociocultural anthropology and describe music building society as a "tribe," in part because its members tend to see themselves as a cohesive group with distinct meta-language, rituals, and values. Whether this analogy is appropriate or not, its use would not be unique in modern anthropology. See, for example, J. McIver Weatherford, *Tribes on the Hill: The U.S. Congress, Rituals, and Realities,* rev. ed. (South Hadley: Bergin and Garvey, 1985).

3. Daniel M. Neuman, *The Life of Music in North India* (Detroit: Wayne State University Press, 1980).

4. See Alan P. Merriam and Raymond W. Mack, "The Jazz Commu-

nity," *Social Forces* 38 (1960): 211–22; Alan P. Merriam, *The Anthropology of Music* (Evanston: Northwestern University Press, 1964), 137–39; Alan Lomax, "Folksong Style," *American Anthropologist* 61 (1959): 927–54, and *Folk Song Style and Culture* (Washington: American Association for the Advancement of Science, 1968); Anthony Seeger, *Why Suyá Sing* (Cambridge: Cambridge University Press, 1988); Christopher Alan Waterman, *Juju: A Social History and Ethnography of a West African Popular Music* (Chicago: University of Chicago Press, 1990); and Bruno Nettl, *The Radif of Persian Music,* rev. ed. (Champaign: Elephant and Cat, 1992), 186–93.

5. The question of social and musical stratification is widely discussed in musical literature. For landmarks, see Max Weber, *Die rationalen und soziologischen Grundlagen der Musik* (Munich: Drei Masken, 1921); Kurt Blaukopf, *Musik im Wandel der Gesellschaft* (Munich: Piper, 1982); John Shepherd, ed., *Whose Music?* (London: Latimer, 1977); and Pierre Bourdieu, *Distinction: A Social Critique of the Judgment of Taste* (Cambridge: Harvard University Press, 1984).

6. Richard A. Waterman, "Music in Australian Aboriginal Culture: Some Sociological and Psychological Implications," *Music Therapy* 5 (1956): 41, 47.

7. See Eunmi Shim, "Taking Lessons and Practicing: The Piano and Tuba Cultures in the School of Music," in *Community of Music: An Ethnographic Seminar in Champaign-Urbana,* ed. Tamara E. Livingston et al. (Champaign: Elephant and Cat, 1993), 107–18.

8. There is a large body of literature dealing with contrastive roles of genders in musical life, seen both interculturally and from the viewpoint of Western music history. See in particular Ellen Koskoff, ed., *Women and Music in Cross-Cultural Perspective* (Westport: Greenwood Press, 1987); and Jane Bowers and Judith Tick, eds., *Women Making Music: The Western Art Tradition 1150–1950* (Urbana: University of Illinois Press, 1986). For discussion of the role of women in vocal music, cross-culturally, see Ellen Koskoff, "When Women Play: Musical Instruments and Gender Style," in [Violet Archer Festschrift] ed. Regular Qureshi and Chris Lewis, in press.

9. In Nettl, ed., *Eight Urban Musical Cultures,* 122–23.

10. Patricia Sandler, "Aspects of Women's Life in the School of Music," in *Community of Music,* ed. Livingston et al., 149–58.

11. Sandler, "Aspects of Women's Life," 150.

12. For a summary of the relevant literature on the origins of music, see Bruno Nettl, *The Study of Ethnomusicology: Twenty-nine Issues and Concepts* (Urbana: University of Illinois Press, 1983), 162–71.

13. Michael Goldstein, *Michail Ignatieff und die Balalaika: die Balalaika als solistisches Konzertinstrument* (Frankfurt: Zimmermann, 1978).

14. College Music Society, *Directory of Music Faculties in Colleges and Universities, U.S. and Canada, 1990–92* (Missoula: CMS Publications, 1990).

15. There are good, practical reasons for the piano's "tyranny." Even so, it is worth noting the significance of the keyboard's structure, with its configuration of white and black keys in the octave, as a major symbol of music—but mainly classical music—on textiles, stationery, posters, jewelry, and whatnot. In this respect the keyboard is matched only by the G-clef and possibly the eighth-note. The notion that a single instrument dominates the curriculum, and that whatever else students learn they must also have ability at the keyboard, is not widely paralleled in other cultures. In the classical music tradition of Iran, for example, there is no similar instrument. Judging from its importance as illustration in theoretical treatises, the oud may, in earlier times, have played this kind of dominant role in Middle Eastern music of the Middle Ages. The drum is the major symbol of Native American music, and in Blackfoot culture, for example, each singer must learn to drum, although there is no curriculum. The closest parallel to the piano may be found in South Indian classical music, in which (at least in formal teaching institutions) all students learn the system by singing, no matter what their final performance medium; virtually all Carnatic musicians have considerable competence as vocalists.

16. Neuman, *The Life of Music in North India,* 164–65.

17. Henry Kingsbury, *Music, Talent, and Performance: A Conservatory Cultural System* (Philadelphia: Temple University Press, 1988), 85–86, deals with the significance of musical lineages, and the principal teacher described in his book is a student of Artur Schnabel. He describes the importance of the studio as a focal point of conservatory society (85–110).

18. This kind of information is readily available in general dictionaries or encyclopedias of music and is thus not explicitly documented here.

19. See Shim, "Taking Lessons and Practicing," 112–14.

20. Heritage and lineage are equally important in Heartland music schools, but the role of the studio is not as central because of the relatively greater importance of the academic aspects of the music curriculum and because of the relationships of music to more traditional academic disciplines.

21. Letter from Edmund J. James, Aug. 1, 1914, Urbana-Champaign, Illinois, published in *Campus Report* 7 (Sept. 1973): 1.

22. Information of this sort is readily available in general music reference books such as Nicholas Slonimsky, *Baker's Biographical Dictionary of Musicians* (New York: Schirmer, 1978); Stanley Sadie, ed., *The New Grove Dictionary of Music and Musicians,* 20 vols. (London: Macmillan, 1980); and H. Wiley Hitchcock and Stanley Sadie, *The New Grove Dictionary of American Music,* 4 vols. (London: Macmillan, 1986).

23. See Bourdieu, *Distinction,* 131–33, for insightful remarks on the relationship of classes and occupations and social mobility.

24. College Music Society, *Directory of Music Faculties.*

Chapter 3: A Place for All Musics?

1. For evenhanded commentary on these matters, see Katherine Bergeron and Philip V. Bohlman, eds., *Disciplining Music: Musicology and Its Canons* (Chicago: University of Chicago Press, 1992), and Rose Subotnick, *Developing Variations: Style and Ideology in Western Music* (Minneapolis: University of Minnesota Press, 1991). The issue of canons is discussed (in a less evenhanded way) in the well-known works of Allan Bloom, *The Closing of the American Mind* (New York: Simon and Schuster, 1987), and E. D. Hirsch, Jr., *Cultural Literacy: What Every American Needs to Know* (Boston: Houghton Mifflin, 1987).

2. See Don Randel in *Disciplining Music,* ed. Bergeron and Bohlman, 15.

3. Ibid., 16–17.

4. Catalogs and bulletins of the respective schools and universities are a source of information on this subject, and my residence in such schools for forty-six years also provides "emic" data of a sort. For more synthetic views, see also Winton U. Solberg, *The University of Illinois 1967–1894: An Intellectual and Cultural History* (Urbana: University of Illinois Press, 1968); Albert Dale Harrison, "A History of the University of Illinois School of Music, 1940–1970," Ph.D. diss., University of Illinois at Urbana-Champaign, 1986; and the autobiography of Indiana University president Herman B Wells, *Being Lucky: Reminiscences and Reflections* (Bloomington: Indiana University Press, 1980).

5. Mark Slobin, "Micromusics of the West: A Comparative Approach," *Ethnomusicology* 36 (1982): 1–87.

6. Ruth Finnegan, *The Hidden Musicians: Music-Making in an English Town* (Cambridge: Cambridge University Press, 1989).

7. For samples and sources, see Richard Schaal, "Konzertwesen," in *Die Musik in Geschichte und Gegenwart,* ed. Friedrich Blume (Kassel: Bärenreiter, 1958), 7:1587–1605. For discussion of concert arrangements and sample programs, see Alice M. Hanson, *Musical Life in Biedermeier Vienna* (Cambridge: Cambridge University Press, 1985).

8. For background and complementary literature, see Peter Manuel, *Popular Musics of the Non-Western World* (New York: Oxford University Press, 1988) and *Cassette Culture* (Chicago: University of Chicago Press, 1993); and Bruno Nettl, "Persian Popular Music in 1969," *Ethnomusicology* 16 (1972): 218–39.

9. But see Tatiana Calhamer, "Shrine, Zoo, Museum, Archive, Lab: A Record Store in Campustown," in *Community of Music: An Ethnographic Seminar in Champaign-Urbana,* ed. Tamara E. Livingston et al. (Champaign: Elephant and Cat, 1992), 15–28.

10. Theodore Grame, "Music in the Jma al-F'na of Marrakesh," *Musical Quarterly* 56 (1970): 74–83.

11. This has been noted in detail, but ascribed to somewhat different causes, by Christopher Small, "Performance as Ritual: Sketch for an Enquiry into the True Nature of a Symphony Concert," in *Lost in Music: Culture, Style, and the Musical Event,* ed. Avron Levine White (London: Routledge and Kegan Paul, 1987), 10–11.

12. One may question the exotic character of gamelans in the context of American institutions. According to an official of the Indonesian embassy charged with keeping such records, in 1992 there were more than two hundred gamelans extant and active in the United States. Rivaling in number the so-called Collegia Musica, gamelans may well be regarded as belonging to and having a standard function in American culture.

13. This issue is touched upon tangentially by many authors who dealt with popular music during the 1980s. See, for example, Lawrence Grossberg, "Another Boring Day in Paradise: Rock and Roll and the Enjoyment of Everyday Life," *Popular Music* 4 (1984): 225–58, and Peter Wicke, "Rock Music: A Musical-Aesthetic Study," *Popular Music* 2 (1982): 219–44. Political bases are usually ascribed to the academic untouchability of rock and country and western by those associated with these genres; adherents of the classical canon ascribe esthetic reasons. See Lawrence Grossberg, *We Gotta Get Out of This Place* (New York: Routledge, 1992), 194–98, and Richard Middleton, *Studying Popular Music* (Milton Keynes: Open University Press, 1990), 103–8.

14. See Randel in *Disciplining Music,* ed. Bergeron and Bohlman, 17.

15. See, for example, Subotnick, *Developing Variations,* and Stephen Blum, Philip Bohlman, and Daniel M. Neuman, eds., *Ethnomusicology and Modern Music History* (Urbana: University of Illinois Press, 1991).

16. For a sampling of relevant literature, see Leonard B. Meyer, *Music, the Arts, and Ideas: Patterns and Predictions in Twentieth-Century Culture* (Chicago: University of Chicago Press, 1967); Carl Dahlhaus, *Grundlagen der Musikgeschichte* (Cologne: Hans Gerig, 1977); and Georg Knepler, *Geschichte als Weg zum Musikverständnis,* 2d ed. (Leipzig: Reclam, 1982).

17. There is virtually no end to the literature of recent years that might be cited to support and illustrate the last three sentences. A variety of viewpoints and approaches include: Joseph Kerman, *Contemplating Music: Challenges to Musicology* (Cambridge: Harvard University Press, 1985); Albrecht Schneider, *Analogie und Rekonstruktion: Studien zur Methodologie der Musikgeschichtsschreibung und zur Frühgeschichte der Musik,* Band 1 (Bonn: Verlag für systematische Musikwissenschaft, 1984); Susan McClary, *Feminine Endings: Music, Gender, and Sexuality* (Minneapolis: University of Minnesota Press, 1991); and Bergeron and Bohlman, eds., *Disciplining Musics.*

18. Bruno Nettl, *Blackfoot Musical Thought: Comparative Perspectives* (Kent: Kent State University Press, 1989), 109–15.

19. See the volumes by Gustave Reese, Manfred Bukofzer, Alfred Einstein, and William Austin in the Norton Series published during the 1940s and 1950s; discussions in *Perspectives in Musicology,* ed. Barry S. Brook et al. (New York: Norton, 1972); Warren D. Allen, *Philosophies of Music History: A Study of General Histories of Music 1600–1960* (New York: Dover, 1962); and, for a sampling of textbooks, see K. Marie Stolba, *The Development of Western Music: A History* (Dubuque: Wm. C. Brown, 1990); Stanley Sadie, *Music Guide: An Introduction* (Englewood Cliffs: Prentice-Hall, 1986); the Prentice-Hall History of Music Series, ed. H. Wiley Hitchcock; and Kenneth Levy, *Music: A Listener's Introduction* (New York: Harper and Row, 1983).

20. See, for illustration, most of the essays in Blum, Bohlman, and Neuman, eds., *Ethnomusicology and Modern Music History.*

21. The literature cited in notes 14 and 15 of this chapter is relevant here as well; see Kerman, *Contemplating Music;* Subotnick, *Developing Variations;* and Bergeron and Bohlman, eds. *Disciplining Music.* The appropriate subject matter of musicology has been an issue for many decades, of course. See, for example, Gustave Reese, in *Perspectives in Musicology,* ed. Brook et al, 11–13, where the accounting of lacunae involves almost exclusively the gaps in our knowledge of early music.

22. Judith Becker, "Is Western Art Music Superior?" *Musical Quarterly* 72 (1986): 341–59.

23. Kerman, *Contemplating Music,* 174; see also Hans Heinrich Eggebrecht, "Historiography," in *The New Grove Dictionary of Music and Musicians* (London: Macmillan, 1980), 8:593.

24. Donald Jay Grout, *A History of Music* (New York: Norton, 1960); the Prentice-Hall History of Music Series devotes roughly equal-sized volumes to the six periods.

25. In the second edition of *Listen* (New York: Worth Publishers, 1976), Joseph Kerman devotes about one-fourth of his space to the twentieth century; four pages within that are on rock music and eight are on "American Popular Music: Jazz." In the sixth edition of *The Enjoyment of Music* (New York: Norton, 1990), Joseph Machlis devotes about 130 of approximately 530 pages to the twentieth century; of this, fourteen pages are on popular styles, and eight are on non-Western music. In the fourth edition of *Music* (Englewood Cliffs: Prentice-Hall, 1988), Daniel T. Politoske devotes about 25 percent (125 pages) to the twentieth century, and within that, approximately twenty-five pages to popular music and jazz; there is a twelve-page chapter on "Aspects of Music in Some non-Western Cultures."

26. The work of the influential music historian Carl Dahlhaus is indicative. In his accounts of the history of Western art music one senses the

central thread of Bach-Beethoven-Wagner-Schoenberg. See his *Die Idee der absoluten Musik* (Kassel: Baerenreiter, 1978), 118–27. But in Dahlhaus's *Foundations of Music History,* translated by J. B. Robinson (Cambridge: Cambridge University Press, 1983), the concept of structural history, essential for the identification of central and peripheral, is subjected to thorough criticism (129–50).

27. These terms were used to distinguish contrastive approaches to the assimilation of minorities, particularly in the distinction of public policy in the United States and Canada. Simple definitions are given in Jean Burnet, "Multiculturalism," *The Canadian Encyclopedia* (Edmonton: Hurtig, 1988), 3:1401. For an early illustration, see Charles Wagley and Marvin Harris, *Minorities in the New World* (New York: Columbia University Press, 1958). The distinctiveness of the Canadian approach in musical context is mentioned in Timothy J. McGee, *The Music of Canada* (New York: Norton, 1985), 105–7.

28. Bruno Nettl, *The Western Impact on World Music* (New York: Schirmer Books, 1985), 149–64.

Chapter 4: Forays into the Repertory

1. Bruno Nettl, *Blackfoot Musical Thought: Comparative Perspectives* (Kent: Kent State University Press, 1989), 124–28.

2. Anthony Seeger, *Why Suyá Sing* (Cambridge: Cambridge University Press, 1988).

3. The question of social and musical stratification is widely discussed in musical literature. See, for example, Kurt Blaukopf, *Musik im Wandel der Gesellschaft* (Munich: R. Piper, 1982); several essays in *Whose Music? A Sociology of Musical Languages,* ed. John Shepherd (London: Latimer, 1977); and, for an earlier classic, Charles Seeger, "Music and Class Structure in the United States," *American Quarterly* 9 (1957): 281–94.

4. J. D. Slotkin, *Menomini Peyotism* (Philadelphia: Transactions of the American Philosophical Society, 1952), 42, pt. 4, 660.

5. For a sample of the relevant literature in music sociology and ethnomusicology, see Ivo Supicic, "Music and Ceremony: Another Aspect," *International Review of Music Aesthetics and Sociology* 13 (1982): 21–38; Ruth Stone, *Let the Inside Be Sweet* (Bloomington: Indiana University Press, 1982); and Seeger, *Why Suyá Sing.*

6. The interpretation of many important events as rituals, and the structural comparison of the rituals in one culture, is an important branch of anthropological and folkloristic literature. One of the major classics is Mary Douglas, "Deciphering a Meal," in *Myth, Symbol, and Culture,* ed. Clifford Geertz (New York: Norton, 1971), 61–82. For a genetic view, see the many works of Claude Lévi-Strauss dealing with ritual aspects of food. For a light-

hearted but insightful comparison of the rituals within one culture, see Nigel Barley, *The Innocent Anthropologist* (London: British Museum Publications, 1983). And for the analysis of concerts as rituals, see Christopher Small, "Performance as Ritual: Sketch for an Inquiry into the Nature of a Symphony Concert," in *Lost in Music: Culture, Style, and the Musical Event,* ed. Avron Levine White (London: Routledge and Kegan Paul, 1987), 6–23.

7. The tradition of "college songs," published in college- or university-specific books, goes well into the nineteenth century. See, for example, *Illini Song Book,* 2d ed (Urbana: Illinois Union, 1926); and *The Northwestern Song Book* (Evanston, Student Body, n.d. [ca. 1900]). For anecdotal history, see Cary Clive Buford, *We're Loyal To You, Illinois* (Danville, Ill.: Interstate, 1952).

8. This American film is based on a novel by Brian Garfield. It was produced in 1980 and directed by Ronald Neame, with Walter Matthau and Glenda Jackson. I am grateful to Dennis Lloyd for pointing it out to me.

9. Walter Wiora, *Das musikalische Kunstwerk* (Tutzing: Hans Schneider, 1983).

10. See in particular Katherine Bergeron and Philip V. Bohlman, eds., *Disciplining Music: Musicology and Its Canons* (Chicago: University of Chicago Press, 1992).

11. See Melinda Russell, "Undergraduate Conceptions of Music," in *Community of Music: an Ethnographic Seminar in Champaign-Urbana,* ed. Tamara E. Livingston et al. (Champaign: Elephant and Cat, 1992), 159–74. An earlier example of ethnomusicological studies in which fundamental musical values were approached through interview or questionnaires of students are Charles and Angeliki Keil, "Musical Meaning: A Preliminary Report," *Ethnomusicology* 10 (1966): 153–73; see also Bruno Nettl, "A Technique of Ethnomusicology Applied to Western Culture," *Ethnomusicology* 7 (1963): 221–24.

12. Christopher Small, "Performance as Ritual: Sketch for an Enquiry into the True Nature of a Symphony Concert," in *Lost in Music,* ed. White, 11–14.

13. There is a great deal of relevant literature, extending from Elias Canetti's belletristic *Crowds and Power* (New York: Viking, 1962), to Richard Norton, *Tonality in Western Culture* (College Station: Pennsylvania State University Press, 1984), to the introductory essay by Stephen Blum in *Ethnomusicology and Modern Music History,* ed. Stephen Blum, Philip V. Bohlman, and Daniel M. Neuman (Urbana: University of Illinois Press, 1990).

Although the audience of classical music in American culture appears to see itself as classless, or broadly middle class, an informal survey of the music accompanying television commercials in 1990–91 suggests a different interpretation. Classical music was used for background in commercials for expensive automobiles, specialty coffees and wines, and gourmet food, products accessible primarily to the upper socioeconomic strata. These apparently old-fashioned and traditional accoutrements of the good life were touted to the strains of Mozart and Bach, whereas other expensive goods such as designer clothes or expensive computing or office machinery were sold via quite different musical styles more associated with the 1980s.

14. Margaret J. Kartomi, *On Concepts and Classifications of Musical Instruments* (University of Chicago Press, 1990).

15. See, for example, Christopher Waterman, *Juju: A Social History and Ethnography of an African Popular Music* (University of Chicago Press, 1990), 38; Paul Berliner, *The Soul of Mbira* (Berkeley: University of California Press, 1978), 1–2, 58; and Stone, *Let the Inside Be Sweet,* 88–90.

16. Bruno Nettl, *The Western Impact on World Music* (New York: Schirmer Books, 1985), 57–60.

17. Soren Kierkegaard, cited in Alfred Orel, *Mozart: Gloria Mundi* (Salzburg: Ludwig Schäffer, 1956), 99–101.

18. Judith Becker, "Is Western Art Music Superior?" *Musical Quarterly* 72 (1986): 341–59.

19. This kind of speculation and analysis is widespread in the literature about Mozart, at least from Alfred Einstein, *Mozart, His Character, His Work* (London: Oxford University Press, 1945), through recent analyses in fiction (Peter Shaffer, *Amadeus* [New York: Harper and Row, 1970] and scholarship such as Peter Csobádi et al. eds., *Das Phänomen Mozart im 20. Jahrhundert: Wirkung, Verarbeitung und Vermarktung in Literatur, bildender knust und in den Medien* (Anif/Salzburg: Ursula Müller-Speiser, 1991).

20. Small, "Performance as Ritual," 7, 9.

21. Something made clear to beginning college students in some of the most venerable texts. See Curt Sachs, *Our Musical Heritage* (New York: Prentice-Hall, 1948), 305.

22. A. R. Radcliffe-Brown, "On Social Structure," *Journal of the Royal Anthropological Institute* 70 (1940): 2–3; Marvin Harris, *Cultural Materialism* (New York: Random House, 1979), 77–115; Alan Lomax et al., *Folk Song Style and Culture* (Washington: American Association for the Advancement of Science, 1968), 133. Of course, the viewpoints of these scholars have never been shared by the entire anthropological profession, but I find them helpful to the endeavor in these essays.

23. Daniel M. Neuman, *The Life of Music in North India* (Detroit: Wayne State University Press, 1980), 28.

24. Nettl, *Blackfoot Musical Thought,* 106, 108, 122. The term is defined in Milton Singer, *When a Great Tradition Modernizes* (New York: Praeger Publishers, 1972), 70–74.

25. Clifford Geertz, "Deep Play: Notes on the Balinese Cockfight,"

Daedalus 101 (1972): 1–37. For examples of "thick" descriptions of musical events in Geertz's sense, see particularly Seeger, *Why Suyá Sing,* and Regula Qureshi, *Sufi Music of India and Pakistan: Sound, Context, and Meaning in Qawwali* (Cambridge: Cambridge University Press, 1987).

26. See Csobádi et al., eds., *Das Phänomen Mozart;* and Richard Taruskin, "Why Mozart Has Become an Icon for Today," *New York Times,* Sept. 9, 1990, H35, H40.

27. See Lee C. Leighton, ed., *The Encyclopedia of Education* (New York: Macmillan, 1971), 1:31–32.

28. Charles Franklyn, "Academic Dress," *The International Encyclopedia of Higher Education* (San Francisco: Jossey-Bass, 1977), 2:23.

Afterword

1. Henry Kingsbury, *Music, Talent, and Performance: A Conservatory Cultural System* (Philadelphia: Temple University Press, 1988).

2. Ellen Koskoff, review of Kingsbury, *Music, Talent, and Performance,* in *Ethnomusicology* 34 (1990): 314, 1990.

3. Kingsbury to the Editor, *Ethnomusicology* 35 (1991): 81–82.

Index

BRUNO NETTL was born in Czechoslovakia in 1930, moved to the United States in 1939, studied at Indiana University and the University of Michigan, and has taught since 1964 at the University of Illinois at Urbana-Champaign, where he is emeritus professor of music and anthropology. Active principally in the field of ethnomusicology, he has done field research with Native American peoples, in Iran, and, secondarily, in Israel and Southern India. He has served as president of the Society for Ethnomusicology and as editor of its journal, *Ethnomusicology*. Among his books are *Theory and Method in Ethnomusicology* (1964), *The Study of Ethnomusicology* (1983), *Blackfoot Musical Thought: Comparative Perspectives* (1989), and the revised edition of *The Radif of Persian Music* (1992).

Books in the Series Music in American Life

Long Steel Rail: The Railroad in American Folksong
Norm Cohen

Resources of American Music History: A Directory of Source Materials from
Colonial Times to World War II
D. W. Krummel, Jean Geil, Doris J. Dyen, and Deane L. Root

Tenement Songs: The Popular Music of the Jewish Immigrants
Mark Slobin

Ozark Folksongs
Vance Randolph; edited and abridged by Norm Cohen

Oscar Sonneck and American Music
Edited by William Lichtenwanger

Bluegrass Breakdown: The Making of the Old Southern Sound
Robert Cantwell

Bluegrass: A History
Neil V. Rosenberg

Music at the White House: A History of the American Spirit
Elise K. Kirk

Red River Blues: The Blues Tradition in the Southeast
Bruce Bastin

Good Friends and Bad Enemies: Robert Winslow Gordon and the Study of
American Folksong
Debora Kodish

Fiddlin' Georgia Crazy: Fiddlin' John Carson, His Real World, and the World of
His Songs
Gene Wiggins

America's Music: From the Pilgrims to the Present
Revised Third Edition
Gilbert Chase

Secular Music in Colonial Annapolis: The Tuesday Club, 1745–56
John Barry Talley

Bibliographical Handbook of American Music
D. W. Krummel

Goin' to Kansas City
Nathan W. Pearson, Jr.

"Susanna," "Jeanie," and "The Old Folks at Home": The Songs of Stephen C.
Foster from His Time to Ours
Second Edition
William W. Austin